# Foreword

*Robbed Without A Gun* though written in fiction format is a powerful tool to call to order what should be a beacon of light to a dark world – the church.

For as long as most African American parishioners can remember, there has been a hint of speculation that all ministers have not and do not live up to the standards that God has outlined in the Bible as it relates to upholding the office of a pastor.

As evidenced by Deborah Smith's hilarious spin of what used to be a horrific experience with an unscrupulous pastor in *Robbed Without A Gun*, once again we faced with the truth, the church has a long way to go, to be the perfect bride Christ seeks to return for.

As individual believers we too find that in our walks with God we struggle to live a life acceptable unto Him. The truth of matter is, we fail and sometimes miserably.

The characters in *Robbed Without A Gun* are flawed beings just like you and me. They are real and grieve when they miss the mark. Though *Robbed Without A Gun* has many moments of laughter, if you have ever struggled with your salvation and the sin that so easily snares mankind, there are plenty of opportunities to shed tears of redemption.

It is my privilege to endorse Deborah Smith's *Robbed Without A Gun* as a delightful, truth-filled novel that is sure to bless many for generations to come.

Blessings and Honor,

Najiyyah Brooks Harris
Co-Founder of True Vine Fellowship Ministries
CEO, True Vine Marketing & Public Relations

# Prelude
## *Looking Back*

Reflecting on my decision to take my two timing husband back - I was *pissed!* I could kick my own self in the rear. If the jerk didn't treat my kitty kat so good I would have never considered letting him come back in the first place. Most of the time when a man's little man is *little*, they will overly compensate with their tongue. Michael was good at using his tongue. It's amazing that he could do something exceptionally well besides lie with that snake that emerges from the hole in his face.

I guess I was very vulnerable. I had previously left Michael, who was the world's biggest cheat and thought that I would be safer in a relationship with a minister. My minister, Pastor Leon Booker, *was just as bad.* He was a liar, a cheat and to top everything off - he lied about being married. Leon treated me good and if I hadn't found out that he was lying to me the whole time, I would have probably stayed with him, after being with broke Michael. The way Leon was *always* throwing money my way I wouldn't have cared about him being married, as long as he kept me in Gucci. What his wife did or didn't do with him would have been her own darn business. He put out the dough unlike Mr. Empty Pockets over here, who wants to come up in the joint destroying stuff and he ain't bought nuthin'. *'Lord, please forgive me I know I'm saved'*, but it seems to be some people's duty to make you lose your salvation. But if the truth be told, I really wanted to fight Michael's a-- !

That no good nigga, had 'stupid' nerve. He walked into our

# Robbed

## WITHOUT A

## gun

## Deborah Smith

***Robbed Without A Gun***
is the highly anticipated sequel
to the widely acclaimed novel

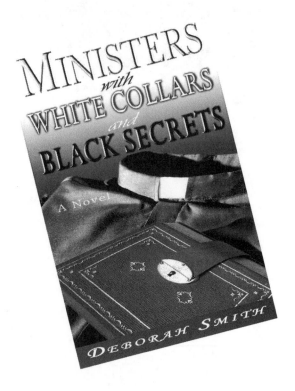

*Ministers With White Collars and Black Secrets*

# *Robbed Without A Gun*
## Deborah Smith

**DEBORAH SMITH PUBLICATIONS**

**Deborah Smith** is available for speaking engagements.
Contact:
True Vine Marketing & Public Relations
P.O. Box 5734
Midlothian, VA 23112
804-683-4280 - Office
804-897-6215 – Fax

## *Robbed Without A Gun*

Copyright © 2004
Deborah Smith Publications

Editor:
Joanie Smith

ISBN: 0-9746136-9-X

1051 Stuyvesant Avenue, #319
Union, NJ 07083
**www.deborahsmithonline.com**

house with a brand new shiny red axe and commenced to slashing our ten thousand dollar custom-made Chinese style bedroom set. He had lost his entire mind. He slashed our 27-inch Plasma Sony television that was mounted on the wall. He was on a marathon slashing everything in sight, outraged because he had gotten caught *again* with yet another one of his trashy hoes.

My cousin Don was upstairs trying to get Hack Saw Jim Duggan (Michael) to calm down and give him the axe. But Michael insisted that he would not give anyone the axe unless I came upstairs to talk with him. *Oh, hell no!* I knew he must've bumped his head on something because I wasn't going nowhere near him or that axe.

Poor Kyasia. It was her 13th birthday party and it must have been at least seventy-five kids at her party. Not to mention the thirty to thirty-five adults there to assist me in throwing my daughter what was supposed to have been the birthday party of a lifetime. But it was this day her stupid a-- father chose to audition for the part of Norman Bates in the movie Psycho and came in here in front of all of her friends throwing a tantrum 'cause he had gotten put out for the last time *or so I thought.*

I can't forget the deranged look formed on Michael's face as he walked down the steps of our 4-bedroom Center Hall Colonial house. He just stared at me with that axe in his hand as he walked out the door. *'He better had taken his sorry a-- out the door 'cause I had already called the cops'.* But on the real, he had me shook.

Everyone was frantic; my daughter was upstairs in her bedroom crying from embarrassment. My sisters were up there along with some of her closest friends trying to console her. My sister Ever Ready was ready for him though, but my oldest sister Queen convinced her to let the men in blue do their job. I, on the other hand, was downstairs trying to calm our guests down. We never got to cut her cake or open her gifts. This was totally the most difficult situation I could imagine myself in.

Anyway, I don't know how, but Leon managed to call me on the worst day of my life. He claimed the Holy Spirit had told him something was wrong. He came to my aid. I really thought he was being concerned about me, but to that lying scoundrel, it was just fair exchange for some good sex. Yes, after all of this bull crap, Ms. Kiyah Simmons has emerged with some really hard earned, '*You Can't Get A Darn Thing Over On Me*' common sense degree. Oh Yes!, I had done backslid all the way.

# Chapter 1
*Confused*

A few months ago, I woke up and realized that my ex-husband had decided to launch his campaign for trying to get me to take him back. This was the beginning of my drama.

I renewed my commitment to God and really wanted to do the right thing. God had restored my salvation and I trusted He was able to restore my marriage. Besides, Michael had been calling and sending flowers to the job.

I was in the office when the large, bouquet of peach roses were delivered with a note that read "I love you and I miss you. PLEASE take me back," it was signed *"Sincerely Yours,"* Michael.

Within minutes the phone was ringing and Sandy yelled, "Kiyah, there is a call for you on line two."

"Thanks Sandy", I replied as I picked up the receiver at my desk.

"Hello, this is Kiyah"

"Kiyah, this is Michael. What's up? Did you get the flowers?"

"Yes."

"So, what's up? Can we get together and talk about working things out?"

"I don't know about working things out Michael, but if you want to talk about giving me some money for your kids, give me a call back later when I'm not so busy in the office."

"What do you mean you don't know about working things out?"

"Just like I said, I'm not working a darn thing out with you. You think that you can go around sleeping with every hoochie in the streets and you expect me to consider taking you back. Humph!, you must be crazy. I know that thing has got to be shriveled up by now," I replied with a smirk on my face.

"When, are you going to get over it Kiyah? WHEN?" Michael said now angry.

"NEVER!"

"I thought you were saved and sanctified, What about our children? Where is your Christianity?"

"Where was your Christianity when you were sleeping with those tramps? Did you think about our children then?" I snapped back.

It disturbs me when people try to throw Christianity up in my face. Just because I'm saved and go to church doesn't mean that I have to stay with someone that is not good for me. Christianity simply means that I have to forgive them. I'm not sure if I have whole heartedly done that, besides he claimed to be a Christian and his salvation didn't keep his zipper closed. So now why does he think it's suppose to open mines? I don't *think* so!

"Look, Kiyah I don't want to argue with you. I really would like to make things right between us, if you would just give me the chance." Michael was pleading his case.

"I'm really busy at work. Thanks for the flowers, but it is going to take a whole lot more than flowers to motivate me into taking you back after ALL you have done," I said while preparing to hang up the phone.

"KIYAH!" Michael yelled into the phone, or at least that's all I heard. I placed the phone on the receiver. CLICK!

What in the world was Michael up to? Why was he so hell bent on getting me back now? Hmmm.... I don't know why he is being so persistent all of a sudden. He's up to something. I know it.

Well I guess when it rains it pours, 'cause after going months without speaking to Leon, here he comes with calling me and sending messages through Paul, his assistant.

Leon and I had broken things off after he preached for the annual Men's Day at my church. Now all of a sudden Leon wanted to see me, but I would be damned if he thought that I was going to turn into one of his little booty calls. But hell,

I must admit, it was tempting, 'cause Leon is the smoothest, finest and classiest man I had ever dealt with. Too bad he wasn't willing to leave his wife. Wow, it's even sadder that I would even *want* him to. *'Lord help me, I don't know what is happening to me.'*

See it had not been too long ago that the effects of my separation from Michael had led me into the arms of Minister Leon Booker, who was everything a woman could dream of, except for the fact that he had lied, about being married. When I found out, I just couldn't trust him anymore.

During this tumultuous time, the Lord had given me a breakthrough. He allowed me to feel His presence and hear His voice. That alone gave me the strength to just let go, walk away from Leon and trust in God. Everything was going fine up until lately - but now I feel so lonely. Sometimes I feel trapped. As a Christian I am only supposed to be intimate with my husband and we're not together. So in the sight of God (if I'm not with my husband), I am sanctioned to just be alone; yet my husband is running around and practically living with another woman.

I prayed, *'Lord I know that you see all things and right now God, I'm cranky, moody and sexually frustrated. Why should I go to sleep every night clutching a pillow tightly between my legs? Why can't I get the thoughts of Leon's hard sculptured caramel golden body out of my head? Lord you've got to help me! I'm feeling so weak right now. I don't think I can hold out much longer. It's not fair that you have given me a conscience when it comes to morals and virtues but failed to provide one to the majority of these no good for nothing, lying men out here namely Michael and Leon....'*

My thoughts were interrupted when Sandy yelled, "Kiyah, you have a call on line two."

I know darn well Michael isn't calling me back already.

"Okay Sandy, thanks," I said as I proceeded to take the call. "Hello, this is Kiyah," I said professionally.

"Sweetheart, how are you?" Leon's familiar voice responded. You know the devil *never* takes a day off. Here I was just thinking about this man and he pops up and calls me after not speaking with him in months.

"Leon, why are you calling here?" I was frantic. I didn't want Sandy to know that Leon was calling me.

"I didn't. I had Paul to call for me, I knew that Sandy would probably answer the phone and I didn't want to put you in an uncomfortable position," Leon was smooth.

*Oooh, he knew me so well. It was amazing.*

"Yeah, so why are you calling now after all of this time?"

"Because I miss you....I can't get you out of my mind. Listen Kiyah, the last past six months have been the most miserable for me....I miss your laughter, your warm and gentle smile, I miss seeing your beautiful face and most of all I miss being with you. Kiyah, I really need to see you."

13

He paused for a moment. I'm thinking '*I know this fool didn't think it would be that easy after he had lied to no end about having a wife.*' Then he continued "Kiyah I am so sorry for lying to you. It's just that I knew if I had told you I was married you would have left me immediately. Seeing as how you are such a virtuous woman, I thought you would leave me immediately considering the predicament I was in." I'm thinking, '*Did he just say WAS?*' He kept rapping, "Sweetheart, I have an obligation to my church and that alone wouldn't allow me to leave my wife. I love you Kiyah....I realize that I am lost without your presence in my life. You make me feel alive again and if nothing else I need your friendship. Please forgive me. I've been vexed without you," Leon said desperately.

I'm thinking. '*Wow! Leon desperate.*' I don't know if I like this side of him. But then again, the man has some strong dough, so now maybe there's a whole lot of opportunity breathing through this phone.

"You know Leon, I understand how you feel, and it was hard for me at first too. But now I'm just getting my life back on track and even though I cared a great deal for you, I can't compromise my integrity and date a married man *knowingly.*" As I was talking to Leon, I thought, '*Too bad Michael's tramp didn't feel that way. She didn't mind sleeping with my husband and ruining my family.*' I spoke to Leon in a soft tone. I didn't want anyone to overhear my conversation, unlike my tone with Michael, when I more or less advertised that I was rejecting him. I wanted everyone to know that Michael was begging to get me back. Especially since he tried to play me the hell out with that low budget chick he was messing around with. Now look at my work: yeah, Leon is a liar, but as far as being a man is concerned - he is the *crème of the crop*.

In the midst of my thoughts, Leon's voice brought me back to reality.

"Okay, Kiyah. I can't do anything but respect that." Leon sounded defeated.

"Leon, I'm really sorry and I sincerely wish you the best. You know you are truly an awesomely gifted person," I tried to make him feel better. Deep down in my heart I believed that Leon really did care about me. He has only ever treated me like a queen. He wined and dined me in the most extravagant restaurants that the Metropolitan Area had to offer.

I remember once mentioning to him that I had a taste for crab cakes. The very next day he had a chauffer take us to downtown Delaware. Before I knew it, we were entering the Brandy Wine Suites Hotel and inside was a very small but elegant restaurant that had the most delicious crab cakes that I've ever had in my entire life. Of course, (after dinner to his convenience) we didn't even have to step one foot outside before making it to a nice king size bed so that he could make a full meal out of me. Leon just had to get compensated for going two and a half hours out of his way by bringing me all the way from North Jersey to downtown Delaware for crab cakes and white wine. Just thinking about that evening of passion with Leon caused the desires in my body to overrule my good *Christian Girl* senses.

Leon's voice interrupted my reminiscing.

"Kiyah, what about dinner? There's nothing wrong with
dinner is it? I still have to retrieve the cell phone I gave
you," he said with a slight chuckle. Leon had given me a cell
phone when we were together; when I broke things off he
stated that he would be coming by to retrieve it. He never
came. Now I know why, this would be his excuse for trying
to see or call me again. This brotha has what you call GCG,
(Good Calculated Game).

Just thinking about all the good times that Leon and I had
shared made me weaken. I was totally crushed when I found
out that he had a wife. I longed for that feeling of hope
and bliss that he provided me with *before* I found out he
had a wife. A *wife!* I will never forget it: when she called
my job and informed me that she was the *wife* of the man,
*the minister* that I had given my body, my time and my
heart to. Then to make matters worse, she wanted to call
me everything that her unstable mind could think of. She
had better be glad that I had more salvation then than I do
now, 'cause I would have cursed her little short, stubby self
out. I can hear her now, with that squeaky voice calling
me all sorts of ungodly things. '*So I'm a scrumpet, huh,
Mrs. Booker? You gonna stick your foot down my throat
huh? Well look at me now, your husband is still calling and
chasing after this scrumpet. So you wanna call me names
and threaten me? BIG MISTAKE. There are just certain
things that you don't do to a DIVA. Watch my work, Mrs.
Booker; payback is a b....!*' Wow! I thought I was over Leon
and the disappointment I felt after finding out his *Black*

*Secret.* But after reflecting on the ugly scene, amazingly, I realized that although the pain was still fresh in my heart and strangely enough I still had feelings for him. Not to mention my weakness for that sexy voice of his; which possesses the power of waking up every nerve in my body.

"You know what Leon….why not? As long as you promise that it's just dinner and nothing more. Sure, we can meet and hopefully we can be friends." *Yeah right, I was weakening. I know just what he wants and I'm going to give it to him.*

"Great! How's tomorrow night?" Leon said excitedly.

Boy, was he anxious.

"That's fine. I'll meet you at the restaurant, *Jezebel's* in midtown Manhattan at seven and don't be late, 'cause I won't wait." I answered as I slammed the phone down. I must at all times keep my diva status even when I'm giving in. But my giving in never requires more than what I'm going to give out - and that will be stress. You see, Mr. Booker is going to have to stretch those pockets a little further this time for these here drawz. *Oh yes, it is definitely more in it for me and this time he won't have to preach these panties off, they'll be coming down only at my convenience.*

I checked my watch and noticed that it's almost lunch time. I called over to Sandy. Sandy was my girl, my honcho. At first we couldn't stand each other but after learning that we had the same experience with the same man, *(yes, Leon)* we became very close.

"Hey, Sandy….where are we going for lunch?"

"I don't know. With all of the calls you've been getting from men today, I thought you might have already had a lunch date," Sandy retorted being a smart aleck. Why should it bother her?

"Whatever! Are we going out for lunch or what?" I asked annoyed.

"Yeah Girl….you're so touchy lately. What's up with you?"

"Nothing, I'm just a little flustered that's all. Have you talked to Miles lately? I haven't heard from him this week and it's already Wednesday and that's not like him," I quickly changed the subject.

Miles is Leon's cousin and he used to work for him. He stopped working for Leon when he found out that Leon had deceived me (telling me he was *not* married and he *was*). We became really close after Leon and I broke up. Miles is fine, six feet 2" and 200 pounds. He's a nicely built piece of butter brown chocolate and has deep dimples resting on both sides of his jaw, which only compliment his almond (Omar Epps) shaped eyes. Of course I thought about a romantic relationship more than once with Miles; and I know he has too. But I thought it would be safer to just keep it at friends. In fact, Miles has become one of my best friends. I think Sandy liked him romantically at one time, but she too has established a friendship with him, so that is too valuable to risk.

"No I haven't talked to Miles since last week; I think he is seeing somebody. He has been quite preoccupied lately," Sandy said with her eyebrows raised.

"*Really?*....good for him," I said unenthused.

"Why don't we, go downtown Newark to Flava's? It's a new restaurant that opened up over there where the old Club America used to be. I heard that the food is really good. The same guy that owns Soul Delicious Restaurant is in charge of the food down there," Sandy explained trying to paint a picture.

"Okay, sure we can go there, I'll see you in about twenty minutes," I said while walking away to my desk.

I don't know why, but all of a sudden I was just irritated in my spirit. As many times as I have joked with Miles about finding himself a mate, the thought of him *actually* being with someone irritated me.

While I was fumbling through some paperwork, I couldn't really focus on anything, so I decided to give Miles a call. When I heard his voice, my mind suddenly eased.

"Hello," he said with that laid back smooth tone of his.

"Hey Miles, what's up? This is Kiyah," I said with excitement.

"I know your voice....What's going on, Kye?"

"Nothing, just calling to check on you, since I haven't heard from you in a minute," I stated while questioning him all at the same time.

"I'm good. Just working and trying to figure what direction I'm going to take my life in," Miles confided now more serious.

"Whoa! Dimples, what's up? Why you digging so deep all of a sudden? I've never heard you talk like this before."

"It's about that time, Kye. I'm really ready to settle down at this point in my life....start a family, a real family.... I got three kids by three different women and they all played me when I was locked up. Three consecutive bids (imprisonments) and three different women that all told me that they would be there for me while I was locked down. Each time, each one of them told me that they were not like the females in my life before them, but they all failed the test of time. Yet, when I was on the streets gettin' money they were all on me. I guess it was never about me though - it was about that cash. Funny, I paid for what other people enjoyed. You feel me?" His hurt and disappointment flowed through the phone.

"It's all good now, I feel you though. Don't worry, the right woman will come along," I tried to make him feel better.

"I know, but when?" He spoke with urgency.

"You just keep the faith. When you least expect, God is going to send you a worthy companion," I answered back.

I really wanted him to find a woman who deserved him, namely me. We have different religious beliefs - but Miles is truly a wonderful person; caring, considerate and *ooooh!* sweet as sweet potato pie ala mode.

"Yeah, aiight. You do that prayin' thing. So ask God to hurry up. I want a family, Kye; I want my kids to live with me so that I can school them the way a father should. I want to see my kids everyday, take them to school and pick them up. You know, conversate with them, so that I can know what's going on in their heads. One day I hope to have a child with a wifey and be with my child from the day that he or she is born, raise them in a home where there is love and truth....I don't like the thought of another man being around and trying to be a father to my kids. I'm here and I want to play my position, but my stupid a-- baby mothas want to give a nigga a hard time, 'cause I don't want to *hit it* (have sex) anymore. They want to be with a nigga when he's on the streets doing good, but bailed out when I was down, HELL NO. Once you cross me ain't no coming back. But I'm going to take care of my kids for sure. Ain't nuthin'. Whatever they need I'm going to get out there and make it happen for mines, *feel me?*" Miles spoke with so much passion it turned me on.

"Wow, Miles. I never knew you were so sensitive when it came to your kids and I definitely didn't think you were into the marriage thing. You seem so thugged out," I said wanting to break the ice. He seemed so upset. Miles talked in such a way, it sent about a million chills up my spine.

"Yeah aiight! I'd show you thugged out if you weren't so

scared of me Ms. Kiyah," Miles challenged with more of a suttle yet serious tone. Deep down inside I *want* him to show me. I *really* wanted and longed for him to show me - But I can't, because he's Leon's cousin. That would be trifling.

"Please. Whatever, Miles. Stop talking to your sister like that. Anyway….are you still taking Kareem to football practice on Saturday for me?" I wanted to steer the conversation in another direction.

"Of course, you know I gotta take my little man to practice. Why don't you let Kareem stay at my joint (house) on Friday? I'm going to have Little Miles with me this weekend anyway."

Miles was so good to my kids. He has always been there for both of my children. Kyasia was a little apprehensive because she didn't want anyone to take the place of her father, but Miles assured her that he just wanted to be her friend. However, Kareem on the other hand, welcomed Miles. He was yearning for the presence of a father figure in his life. You would think that their daddy was dead, but that's just his brain (dead). He lives within minutes of his children, but he doesn't call often or spend anytime with his son. Thank God for Miles. Now if he would just get saved, he would make someone a wonderful husband.

"No problem. What time do you want me to drop Kareem off?" I asked

"Know what? Put his things in his book bag. I got his football gear already at my joint (house) so I might as well pick him up from school. And I'll get Kyasia from her school too and drop her off at your house, or if she wants she can roll with us to get sumthin' to eat. This way you can get a little break for a change. Use this time to go get yo' nails did or sumthin'," Miles laughed.

What would I do without him? He's my best friend. Wish I had married a man like him.

"That's sound great, thank you boo. You know I might just have to take you up on that other offer one day after all," I teased letting him know our possibility.

"What other offer?" Miles was puzzled.

"You know - the one about you showing me just how thugged out you can be," Giving him my sexy tone, I answered.

"Baby Girl, you don't want to do that; you'd be getting yourself into something you can't get out of."

"Why would I want to get out?"

"You wouldn't - feel me? Yo' but listen don't play yourself 'cause you know I ain't never hid the fact that I was wit it. You was always bull crapping talking all that Jesus stuff. Jesus wants you to be happy, don't he Kye?" Miles asked sounding annoyed.

"Look Miles, I don't know. You are a wonderful person, but you're Leon's cousin and I know that Sandy has feelings for you too, and besides she's my good friend. You and I are the best of friends and a relationship between the two of us could just ruin everything," I back peddled trying to convince myself.

"This is about you and me, not everybody else. And yo', listen - Leon ain't my real cousin that's just some old school sh--....our families were raised together so we just always called each other cousins....that motha f---a ain't my real family," Miles said with a very irritated tone.

"Darn, Miles; why you never told me that before?" I said surprised.

"'Cause there was no need. We don't politic about Leon.... and for one - I don't have time to be building with a female talking about the next brotha. *You feel me*? That ain't me," he snapped.

"Okay, calm down. Well listen....I'm going to talk with you later or either I'll see you on Saturday when you bring Kareem home. Sandy is just about dancing in the doorway 'cause she is ready to go eat," I said trying to get off the phone, but Sandy was really in the doorway huffing and puffing 'cause she had been waiting for about five minutes.

"Okay Baby Girl, I ain't gon' keep waitin' for you to find some heart. I'll talk to you later," he said as he was preparing to hang up.

"Oh! Is that right?" I said surprised.

"You heard me but yo', I'ma let you go 'cause I need to get some rest anyway before goin' to work tonight."

"Okay, see you later," I barely said.

"Aiight, peace." Miles hung up.

As I was walking down the aisle heading out of the office, I was thinking....Miles sure is a good catch. He's loyal, strong, caring and fine! If I wasn't so terrified of getting into something real again, maybe I really would consider Miles. In the far distance I sincerely believe that he has that genuine love, concern and understanding that would allow us to build a relationship wealthy in happiness instead of materialistic things. But for now - I'm going to play it safe. After everything I have been through, I can't risk being robbed again....

## Chapter 2
### *Afternoon Service*

My thoughts were interrupted with Sandy yelling.

"Girl what's wrong with you? Why are you walking around here in a daze all of a sudden?"

Sandy was curious. So to throw her off, I answered quickly.

"Nothing, there's nothing wrong with me. I'm sorry for keeping you waiting. Are you ready to go?" I said coming back to the real world.

I headed towards the ladies room, with Sandy in tow. I wanted to freshen up. You know....make sure my 'diva' profile was in tact.

"Yeah, I'm ready, but I wish you would tell me what's been bothering you lately....All of the calls today and now you're practically daydreaming.....Are you sure you're okay?" Sandy was hammering at the issue. I was about to respond to Sandy's accusations when a familiar voice echoed out of the bathroom yelling.

"And more importantly, *who* were you on the phone with?" Benita insisted as her body followed her voice out of the ladies room.

"None of your business, Ms. Nosiness" I wondered how she could hear our conversation from in the bathroom.

Needless to say, we hadn't even opened the door to go inside yet. Now, I know my office was close to the bathroom, but was it that close? It didn't surprise me at all, because Benita's antennas (ears) are powered by satellites and over the years her nosiness has increased in power. Benita is my sister-in-law, my oldest brother Wali's wife and she has no shame when it comes to other folk's business.

"That's, okay; you don't want to tell ole' Benita nuthin' anymore. Before you and Sandy became so coochie crunch, you used to tell me everything. But that's okay, you're gonna need me one day and I'm not going to be around. That's quite alright Kiyah, I'm gonna fix you both. So you want to keep the good dirt from ole' Benita, huh? Don't worry, you two are going to want to know something from me and you know that Benita's got the Metropolitan area covered when it comes to church folk gossip….so what's up?" Benita persisted laughing at first and then she got serious. "No, for real Kiyah, I mean what's really up? What is going on with you Kiyah? I heard you in there on the phone talking about marriage and a relationship ruining everything. You betta talk to me," Benita said acting like a big sister.

"Girl, you only heard one side of the conversation with your nosy self. I was giving a friend some advice," It was an attempt to dismiss her accusations and then I switched it up. "Sandy and I are going downtown to Flava's to get something to eat, want to come?"

"Oh no…..Did you two forget that on Thursday's we have noon day service? I'm going upstairs to get my blessing. If

27

you want to be kept, you better stay in the presence of the Lord. The Word is the only thing that's going to keep you in these last and evil days, *Hallelujah!* With these gangs all around killing innocent people just for membership requirements, the Lord has saw fit to keep me in the midst of it all. I'm not going to miss one opportunity to praise Him. I thank God for His mercy....*Thank you Jesus!* Whew! I can't help it, I get excited about where God has brought me from.....I'll see y'all later." Benita cut a little step before going over to the elevator that led upstairs to the main sanctuary.

Sandy and I stood there looking at Benita and laughed. Suddenly Sandy stopped laughed and said,
   "Kiyah, why don't we go upstairs to service? We can go down to Flava's tomorrow." She was feeling guilty by what Benita had said.

'Why, did Benita have to start her mini sermon with us today?!'
   "Okay, I guess Benita is right," I said reluctantly.

   We put our coats back in the office and then we went upstairs to the sanctuary. As we headed towards the sanctuary I could hear the praise team singing "God Is". Once I entered the sanctuary and sat in the back I could here the words clearly, *'....God is the joy and center of life. He moves all pain, misery and strife. He promised to keep me, never to leave me, He's never ever come short of His Word.* **I've got to fast and pray to stay in His narrow way.'**

Just hearing this song made me think. *'Maybe that's*

*when the problems came in with the maintaining of my salvation....When I stopped fasting and praying like I should. That's when all of those sexual desires started creeping up on me.'* The bible says that *"These things will only come out through prayer and fasting."* *These things - meaning the very things that we need God to protect us from, so that we can keep the mind and the ability to live holy and just.* Since I stopped fasting every Wednesday I am now struggling to control my desire for intimacy with a man.

*'Lord you've got to help me. I don't want to feel the things that would cause me do something that would not be pleasing in your sight. But God I can't focus on fasting and praying lately. Leon is now calling me once again and Michael wants to get back with me and make our marriage work. The children would love that. What should I do with my flesh? I haven't been with a man in six months and my body is aching for that touch. Yet I know if I make that move it would not be honorable in your sight. Lord I want to do what is right, but these feelings keep rising up in me and I know that it is only a matter of time before I give in to them'*

*"Lord Help!"* I whispered as I was taking my seat. Already my tears were falling. Although I had alot of thoughts running through my head and alot of needs that needed to met, I couldn't say anything but just, *"HELP!"* I didn't realize it, but immediately I was overtaken by the Spirit of God that was already in the sanctuary. Sandy looked at me strange as if to say, 'What are you crying for?' I thought to my self 'It's a broken thing you wouldn't understand.' I was crying because I was still broken from abusive and

disappointing relationships. I had been broken because I compromised my virtues for the sake of having a man. God had healed me six months ago from all of this, but today I realized that the bandages were beginning to fall off of the bruises and the sores were still there. I didn't want to loose my connection with Him (God) once again. Yet I felt *driven* by that desire, that burning desire to be touched and caressed by a man. That intense desire kept me clutching my pillow between my legs every night. It was powerful and demanding calling me like a mighty rushing wind.

My thoughts were interrupted when the minister for that afternoon began speaking out prophetically. With his intriguing voice he spoke out saying, **"Somebody has been pushing and it seems that the more you push the worst it gets, but God has sent me here to tell you on today to KEEP ON PUSHING and that door, that stubborn door is going to BUST WIDE OPEN."**

Somehow I knew that God had sent that message especially for me. I just knew it, but I really didn't want to hear this now because I had a date with Leon, Michael was trying to work things out with me and I didn't want to be committed to living right at this time. I cared for Michael deep inside, (only because he was the father of my children) but I didn't like his ways. I would only be taking him back for the sake of the children and would never be true to him again, because I had a payback spirit in my heart and I knew this wasn't of God. Then on the other hand, there was Leon: he was everything I could have imagined my perfect companion to be - except for the fact that he was married. I wanted him back again in the worst way. He made things rise up inside of me that I thought were dead and buried. This was madness. I am just so confused.

The man of God was prophetically speaking. He was going up and down the aisles calling several people out and speaking a WORD to them. Then he came up the middle aisle and stopped at my row, pointed at me and then called me out.

"Sister, come here" he said with authority. My knees got weak. Why in the world did he have to put me on the spot, out of all of the people in the sanctuary?!

As I was making my way out the aisle he was extended his hand to help me. He grabbed my hand and pulled me out into the aisle in front of him. Continuing to hold my hand, he closed his eyes and began to speak. **"Hallelujah, Thank you Jesus. I hear the Spirit of the Lord saying that you need to turn it over to Jesus....Thank you Lord, and uh....I hear the Lord saying that you thought you were delivered, but you're still hurting and you now want to take matters into your own hands."** He paused for a moment and then opened his eyes. Looking directly at me, he squeezed my hand tightly and spoke. **"....GOD wants you to know today my sister that THE BATTLE IS NOT YOURS, IT'S THE LORD'S."**

I knew that he was right, but I didn't know where to begin. I thought I was delivered when God brought me out of that relationship with Leon, but it seems that lately that desire has intensified seven times over.

*'LORD HELP ME. But not right now because there are some insatiable desires that I have to satisfy before*

*recommitting to you.'* I wanted to be saved but then again I wanted to do things that weren't right.

Out of pure confusion I started getting emotional. I was feeling convicted by the message, but yet and still, not convicted enough to change my mind. I was already settled on the fact that I was going to see Leon for dinner and who knows what else. Who am I trying to fool? It must be myself 'cause I sure can't fool God. God knows that **I wanted Leon to tackle my kitty kat like it was carrying the ball in the final seconds of the 4th down with the score tied and within yards of a win for a Superbowl Championship.** Why do I have to know better? Why can't I go out there and have pre-marital sex like the rest of the world and not feel guilty?

I didn't realize that I was still standing in the center aisle until I felt the minister touching me. He had his hand on my forehead and he was praying for me. I remember hearing him say, **"Devil you are liar. This child belongs to God. She wants to do right, but evil is always there. Lord you said that you would keep us if we want to be kept. Keep her Lord God, dispatch Your angels to encamp around about her and protect her from the enemy who is seeking whom he may devour. Your Word says that You would rebuke the devour for our sakes. So today Lord, Hallelujah!....we know that You honor Your Word so we believe it is done right now! Thank you Jesus! Help her Lord, Hallelujah! Amen and amen!** Once he finished praying for me, he hugged me and oh my God! - did he smell good? Then I noticed that he was a *very* nice looking brother. As I tried to return to my seat, he grabbed my right

arm to stop me and said    "Sister, help is on the way, God
has not forgot." He walked back up the aisle towards the
pulpit where one of the church nurses was waiting with
a glass of water and a handkerchief for him. Funny, how
Sister Sharon can act like a nurse and stand there anxious
to help the guest minister. She has nursed every 4$^{th}$ Sunday
for two years and has only barely stayed for the completion
of the sermon to assist our own ministers. Just look at
her refilling his glass and offering him more. I could just
slap her up there trying to act like she is so hospitable. I
know she's only doing that because he is young and good
looking. Could it be that her *'kat'* was purring too? Once
he sat down Sharon finally stopped filling his water glass.
Thank God, because I thought Sharon was going to drown
the man. It is amazing how a good looking black man can
raise your level of service and so quickly. That phony trick,
*I know I shouldn't be calling names in church* but by now
she (Sharon) had gotten on my last nerve. I was relieved
when she found her dignity and sat her desperate self down
somewhere.

Finally, my brother Jared got up to extend the altar call.
He started off by thanking Minister Sean Johnson for the
wonderful sermon and he elaborated by saying "I would
like to thank you my brother for reminding all of us here
today that **God has not forgot, God has not forgot about
my tears, God has not forgot about my heartaches, GOD
has not forgot about my brothers that are on drugs,
God has not forgot about my children that are facing
dangers seen and unseen everyday. I don't care what
you are going through today church, GOD HAS NOT
FORGOT."**

I'm thinking, '*here we go.*'

Why couldn't Jared allow Minister Sean to be the only one to deliver a sermon on *this* afternoon? Preachers kill me it's like the *playoffs* up in here. Or should I say the *show offs*. They're always trying to out do each other. You ask them to give remarks and they want to preach a sermon. Why does Jared have to go and re-preach? '*Lord please let Jared sit down, I'm hungry.*'

But I guess God didn't answer that prayer 'cause Jared just continued shifting into his preaching mode.... **"He said that if you walk upright before me, I will withhold no good thing from you. Just because you took time out and came here today, there is a blessing in store for you. You could have been at Red Lobster, you could have been at Wendy's, you could have been at McDonald's - but you decided to come here and bless the name of Lord today. God is going to honor your sacrifice. Thank you Jesus! Because of your sacrifice, God is going to remember your silent tears, God is going to remember your heartaches and pains, God is going to remember the things that you have been praying and fasting for. God is going to remember your children. God is going to remember your spouse. God is going to remember your loved ones while they're walking in the midst of danger.** Jared paused as the sanctuary was in an uproar. The people were praising God and there was a sweet spirit in this place. You could hear the weeping of some and the anguish in others and they were crying out, *"We love you God, We praise You God, Hallelujah, Thank you Jesus, You've been so Merciful,*

*You've been so Good, Thank you Jesus."*

Everyone seemed to be enjoying Jared, but I wanted him
to sit down - now this was not of God. This is what you
call grand larceny - up in here stealing folk's time like
this. Jared knows he's supposed to be making the altar call
and not recalling people's attention to another sermon.
But I guess I was the only one in the sanctuary that felt
that way. Because when I took my hand off my hip and
looked around everybody and I mean *everybody* in there
was praising and thanking God something awful. Scared
me too! At first 'cause I felt like I was in the twilight zone.
Then a thought came.... 'Maybe I'm the devil. Everybody
in here is in the Glory of God and I'm totally removed from
it all.' Quickly I closed my eyes tight and tried to get into
Jared's sermonette....    **"Your breakthrough is on the
way and the key is in praising Him. See God inhabits
the praises of His people, so if you're going through
something that you can't seem to find your way out of,
all you have to do is PRAISE HIM. The Bible shows
us that where-ever Jesus walked here on earth; nothing
could remain dead in his presence. So if you want
God to show up - Praise Him. If you're going through
something and the more you pray - the worst it gets,
that situation just seems dead - all you got to do is give
God a sacrificial praise and I declare He's going to show
up and show out. And when God shows up, something
dead has got to be revived. When GOD shows up, LIFE
automatically comes with him. I don't care how dead
your situation is, God is able to resurrect it. Is there
anything to hard for God? NO! He can do anything but
fail...."** As Jared was exhalting most of the people were

taking to the aisles dancing, falling out, crying and praising God. He tried to stop them. "Y'all betta sit down 'cause the more you praise Him, the more something keeps leaping in my spirit. See I was suppose to come up here and give the altar call **but when I think of the goodness of Jesus and ALL that he has done for me - something happens. I get like Jeremiah. It becomes like FIRE shut up in my bones. I was a drug dealer, a womanizer, an alcoholic, I don't know about you, but I should have been dead but GOD...."** That's all Jared could say before he broke into a *'shout'* on the pulpit, and then it was like a wave. The minister that spoke this afternoon jumped up and started dancing unto the Lord. Brother Junior, who was on the organ, had to stop playing. Before you knew it, he was up off the organ and giving God an awesome praise. All you heard was the drums and the praises, the drums and the praises. *'Boom! Boom! Hallelujah! Boom! Boom! Jesus, Glory! Hallelujah! Boom! Boom!'*

For some reason I looked at little Brother Jay-Jay as he was playing those drums. It seemed like he was praising God in his playing. Surely the Lord was in this place, yet I couldn't feel Him. The tears began to fall, because I knew deep down inside that it was because of me. I didn't feel Him because I still wanted to do my own thing - go out with Leon, lusting and contemplating my own sexual desires. It's an awful, empty feeling to know that God is in the midst and not be able to feel him. Once you've experienced the presence of God in your life and encountered the Holy Spirit, the joy unspeakable is inexpressible. Jared had finally contained himself and officially gave the altar call. Seven people came to Christ, he then extended an invitation for the backsliders.

I know that I should have been the first one up there, but I couldn't. How would that look the Pastor's daughter going up and admitting she had fallen back on God?

Before you knew it service was over and I finally found Sandy two rows up laid out and slain in the Spirit. I helped her up and took her outside the sanctuary where they were passing out lunches. While I was standing there fanning Sandy, the young minister came out of the sanctuary to go in the back study to change.

Jared yelled to me, "Kiyah do you have your keys to let Minister Sean in the back to change?" Wow, Sean was a cutey. This was a grand opportunity for me. Now just as I was about to get my keys out of my bag, sanctified Sandy started yelling and crying again, "Thank you Jesus! Thank you Jesus!" Some of the ushers had to come over and help me to calm her down.

Jared turned around and said, "That's alright Kiyah. Take care of Sandy. I'll ask Deacon Williams to let him in."

Oooh! I was mad! Sandy was holding onto me crying. I pried her tentacles from around my shoulders and sat her right back down. I ought to bust her in her head. She just always has to over do it. Service has been out for over five minutes and she has to be the only late bloomer in the building. The Holy Ghost had flown itself throughout this place for the last 55 minutes and she decides to catch it now, while I had the opportunity to be of service to this handsome, young, and good smelling prophet of God. *I know I'm not right.*

Immediately after Deacon Williams had escorted Minister Sean in the back, Sandy finally calmed completely down.

"Kiyah, God is so good. Aren't you glad we decided to come up here for service?" Sandy said with an exhausted voice.

"Yeah I'm glad we came for service. But why did you have to start shouting all of a sudden when Jared was asking me to take that preacher to the back to change? Did you see him? Girl, he is fine," I whispered to Sandy. Sandy just stood there with her hands on her hips and looking me up and down.

Then she sucked her teeth and stated "That's exactly why I started shouting to keep you from getting yourself into trouble once again."

OH NO! She didn't.

"Sandy, I know you didn't put on that grand performance just to stop me from getting the chance to be alone with Minister Sean?"

I was annoyed and amused at the same time.
    "Oh yes I did, 'cause you can't help yourself. Haven't you learned your lesson with Leon? Don't be pathetic. Girl, the last thing you need right now is another minister in your life," she scolded.

"Sandy, God is going to get you. You shouldn't play with

the Holy Spirit like that."

"I wasn't playing heifer. I felt the Holy Spirit, I just decided to get a little loud with it that's all," Sandy said chuckling.

"Okay, whatever girl. We only have about 5 minutes left before we have to go back to work and everyone is already gone. Let's go to the ladies room and freshen up," I said wanting to change the subject.

As we were talking and fixing our faces in the mirror, a voice came out from one of the stalls.

"Kiyah I know you don't have your eyes set on that minister." Mid sentence I knew it was Benita. All of a sudden she came out of the stall laughing. "Uh huh, I knew you both would be in here talking right after service, especially since a young handsome minister had entered the building. I knew it, that's why I'm the 'queen of gossip' because I have a keen sense of gossip finding ability." Benita was acting like she had solved the world's greatest mystery.

"Alright Benita, I think he's really cute," I admitted.

"Yeah, he is cute," Sandy agreed.

"What's with all this cute stuff? Y'all grown women, that man is fine." Benita said, "Get him Girl."

"Benita, I don't know what you're talking about. I'm not chasing after no man. He's good looking and all, but I've never been a chaser and I'm not starting now," I shot back.

"Yeah right, Kiyah. I've known you since before you knew yourself....You might not be no man chaser, but you've always had a way of getting what you wanted....The only problem was that you never realized what you were getting yourself into." Benita was coming down my street and it was hitting home. Why did she have to go there?

Ooooh.... if I didn't have so much respect for her, I would read her like the New York Times. I definitely wanted to let her have it, but I'm going to play it cool and let her slide for now.

"Benita, do you know that God has given you an awesome gift?" I asked.

"Yes," she replied.

"God has rewarded you for your faithfulness," I continued.

"Yes....Hallelujah. He has," Benita quickly replied.

"You can see what others cannot. God has equipped you with this ability," I continued.

"Yes Sir. Thank you, Jesus. He sure has," Benita interrupted.

"You encourage me because your life exemplifies your salvation." I said raising my hand to sky.

"Yes Lord!" Benita yelled.

"Your life is an example of how our Christian walk should be." I continued now with a preaching tone. As I looked over at Sandy she to was in the Spirit a little bit shaking her head from side to side whispering 'thank you Jesus'.

"Yes, to God be the Glory," Benita yelled with both hands raised.

"You are holy, because he is holy. You don't drink, because God has delivered you from it."

"He-e-e-y! thank ya' Lord, thank ya' for your deliverance," Benita shouted while jumping up and down.

"You don't smoke anymore, you don't wear red lipstick anymore, you don't sleep with married men anymore - because God has delivered you and gave you a husband that you can be with. God did it all so that your life can be a testimony of His greatness." I spoke with a real live preaching tone so convincing that I surprised myself.

"Hallelujah, thank you God, thank you Jesus." Benita was dancing all over the bathroom and even Sandy was bent over praising God.

I stopped Benita, held her hands and told her to look at me, because I had a Word from the Lord. Immediately she stopped and whispered, "Yes Lord, yes Lord."

"Benita the Lord is saying that if YOU DON'T STOP

WITH YOUR NOSINESS AND STOP WORRYING
ABOUT OTHER FOLK BUSINESS, HE'S GOING TO
STOP WORRYING ABOUT YOUR BUSINESS." I laughed
after I got all the words out. Benita didn't find it funny at
all. But Sandy was dying.

"Kiyah, you think that's funny, but God is going to get you,
lying on Him like that. God is not mocked." Benita said as
she gathered her things to leave the restroom.

"I'm sorry, Benita. I was just playing. *Lord, please forgive
me*," I said looking up toward the ceiling. Yelling after
Benita, I continued, "But you've got to stop it with your
nosiness; hiding in bathroom stalls, sneaking around trying
to find out other folk's business. What kind of mess is that?"
I said as I was grabbing my purse to run behind Benita.

As I made my way out to the foyer, who was coming out
of the door that leads to the studies? Nobody, but Minister
Sean.

"Excuse me, Sister Kiyah. I'm Minister Sean Johnson and
your brother Minister Jared told me that you were his sister,"
he said with that oh so distinctive voice of his.

"Yes, I am" I answered.

"I hope that you take heed to the Word of the Lord. God
wants to do a mighty work in your life and it would be a
shame for such a beautiful young lady such as yourself to be
led astray." He looked at me, very intensely but not lustful.

"What makes you say that I'm being led astray?"

"That's the Holy Ghost. God has given me that gift to see these things," he said cautiously

*I just hope the Holy Ghost is not revealing the attraction that I am experiencing for him right now.* "Minister Sean, you just continue to pray for me. The devil is constantly busy. I will admit that," I said as I was extending my hand to him. "My name is Kiyah Simmons. I'm single, saved and pleased to formally meet you in the name of Jesus."

He smiled as he wrapped both of his hands around mine and replied, "Well, it's nice to formally meet you, Ms. Kiyah Simmons and for the record - I am single and saved as well."

Sandy was standing by the elevator that leads back downstairs to our offices, waving behind his back gesturing for me to come on. But I gave her a look that said *Girl you better go on about your business.* See I could come back late from lunch; this was my dad's church. She on the other hand - could not. So, she took my hint reluctantly and went on downstairs.

When the elevator door closed and Sandy was totally out of sight, Minister Sean made his move. "Kiyah, would you like to go out for dinner or a movie or something.... maybe Saturday early evening?" he asked nervously.

"What? My schedule is very hectic this weekend but...."
I said as I opened my red Gucci bag, (which by the way I

also had on the shoes to match), to give him my business card. Minister Sean couldn't take his eyes off of me and I didn't blame him. I had to admit it to myself, I was sharp. I had on my gray Tahari tailored made skirt suit that was thinly trimmed in red, accented with my red Gucci bag and shoes to match. My hair was upswept in a messy but sexy ponytail held together by a scrunchie made out of red and gray feathers and some of my long strands of hair fell around my caramel colored face on purpose.

I need to be ashamed of myself, standing here profiling and flirting with Minister Sean, wearing from head to toe gifts from Leon.

"Here you go Minister Sean. My contact numbers are listed on there," I said as I handed him my business card.

"Thank you. Here's mine," he handed me his.

"Great, I need to get back to work. I guess I will talk with you soon," I said giving him the 'LLD' you know the 'Light Let Down' the one that says: you missed the basket on this one, but let this other brother foul me and you will advance to the line for another shot.

"Yes, you will. You definitely will....take care Kiyah and God bless you." He began to walk towards the steps that led outside the building.

"You too and God bless you," I said as I made my way over to the elevator to go downstairs.

As I was riding downstairs, I couldn't help but think about Minister Sean. He was gorgeous, tall about six feet with a very light complexion and a beautiful smile. He must weigh no more than 210 pounds and very sculptured. His naturally jet-black curly hair was cut very close and his sideburns and hairline were outlined sharply. He looked so clean cut in his suit. I know Armani when I see it and his cufflinks declared 'Barney's New York.' His scent was Boucheron, (one of my favorite colognes), not to mention that he is single, (at least so far he's single.) I've really got to make up with Benita now. I have to put her on the case to make sure that *he's single and his wife is too.* I'm not taking any more chances. But if he *is* single *"what a man, what a man, what a mighty good man."* I sung in a whisper as I walked back into the office.

As I walked pass Sandy's desk, she rolled her eyes at me like she didn't want to be bothered. You think I cared? I went on the other side of the office to visit and make up with Benita, who gave me the hand before I could get ten feet within her desk.

"Talk to the hand, 'cause I don't look demons in the face," Benita yelled out with her back to me.

"Come on Benita, I was just kidding with you upstairs," I pleaded.

"It's all right to play with me, but it's an abomination to play with God like that. All jokes aside...." she paused and turned around to face me. She scared me because for once Benita was totally serious. "Kiyah, what is going on with you lately? I see you slipping and I can't understand it. God delivered you. I was there when you got your breakthrough. I know what you've been through with the men in your life, I was right there. I know behind that pretty face and glamour girl smile is a severely hurt woman. Don't take matters into your own hands, TRUST IN GOD. He is able to mend your heart. I know you didn't mean anything by your little prank upstairs but I'm a little overly sensitive now Kiyah. I guess you couldn't have known 'cause I haven't told anyone that I'm sick," Water began to swell in Benita's eyes.

"SICK! Benita why didn't you tell me? Sick with what?" I said alarmed.

"Kiyah I have cancer, lung cancer." Benita was whimpering.

"Oh no, Benita. I'm sorry. What can I do to help?" I said now feeling so guilty for playing with her the way I had upstairs. I started dropping a few tears and as I did Benita wiped them and held onto my face. Benita was about 20 years older than me: She must be about 52, yet she's still very shapely and attractive.

"Kiyah, the only thing you can do for me is trust in the Lord and lean not to your understanding….I'm going to be okay, The Lord didn't bring me this far to leave me, but I need for you to be careful and stop massaging your heartaches and trying to heal your love wounds with another man…Don't you see that the devil is using your weaknesses as a tool to *rob* you of the blessings that God has in store for you….just be faithful to Him. Be faithful to God. He will send you a mate. You don't have to go looking for him. The bible says that "whoso findeth a wife, findeth a good thing...." Trust God, Kiyah and always know that I sneak around and try to keep up with your business because I love you and I need to make sure that you're okay," Benita said hugging me.

I loved her too, God knows I do. She is just like my real sister.

I knew she was right and I couldn't help but cry as she was holding me. I know that God was able to do exceedingly and abundantly above all that I could ask or think, but I couldn't help myself. I know for a fact that God doesn't need my help, but still I sign up for overtime everyday trying to help God do His job. Immediately I started praying in my spirit *'Lord I don't know what's wrong with me lately. Doggonit! I am attracted to every decent looking man I see. I don't want to be like this. I just want to find the right man that will: love, respect, honor and treat me the way that I deserved. Lord, I know that I shouldn't desire to have sex before marriage. I know that it's wrong and again Lord, I need your help because just like my shoes, I need to try them on before I buy them....Father HELP!'* I was crying for Benita. I was crying for myself.

Afterwards, Benita gave me more details as to the extent of her condition and it worried me. However the most intriguing element was the fact that she seemed more concerned with my emotional stability than her own physical health. Wow, that's love for you.

By the time I left Benita's desk, Sandy's attitude had evaporated and she was suddenly speaking to me once again. She inquired about what Benita and I were discussing and wanted to know what I had planned for later. Little did she know I had too many plans - all of which included men. Leon was taking me out to dinner tomorrow and who knows how Michael will fit into this picture. Even though I can't stand him, he's still my husband and of course this makes him the only one in the sight of God that should scratch my itch. Oh yes, my plate is full. I need to pick up the kids, feed them, go over homework and prepare them for bed. Then I have to take my time and determine just what my wardrobe for this power packed weekend will consist of.

## Chapter 3
*Leon's Back*

Friday night came before I knew it. Michael was picking Kyasia up to spend the weekend with him. He seemed a little upset when I told him that Kaseem was spending the weekend with Miles, who was going to take him to football practice on tomorrow morning. Michael made himself totally clear telling me that from now on he would take Kaseem to practice on Saturdays. Then he shocked me by saying *that he guess it's his fault that another man is doing what he should have been doing for his son.* Michael assured me that he is sorry for not helping me in the past with our children, but since he has accepted Christ into his life (FOR REAL - so he says), this time, from now on, he is going to be the father that he is supposed to be. Since our separation he hadn't spent much time with the kids. This was is way of punishing me and/or making sure that I didn't have much time to spend with someone else. Although he sounds convincing I'm still skeptical. Michael has pretended to be save more times than I care to remember. But, this time seems a bit more genuine. But trust and understand, I'm not quick to believe him. I'm just going to watch him and see how long it takes him to find a phone booth to change from Super Dad back to Super Jerk. But in the meantime while he's campaigning to win me back, he's providing me with a weekend of freedom to finally have some time to myself. Little does he know that I'm going to use this time to free up some things *that's been locked away for far too long.* Lord, help me. My body is already tingling from the anticipation of seeing Leon after almost 6 months.

I chose to rock: a moderately low cut, no sleeve, black
Max Studio dress, made out of a very rich, clingy jersey
sort of material. This dress just draped over me, nicely
accentuating every curve. See this was my 'make him bite
his knuckles dress'. I threw a black scarfish type of shawl
around my shoulders that matched the material of my dress
perfectly, which I had luckily picked up at Macy's about a
week earlier. It was approximately 6:15 p.m. when I was
standing in front of my bedroom mirror fully dressed and
drenching myself in the Escada perfume that Leon had given
me on our first official date. I sprayed my neck, behind my
ears, my wrist and up underneath my dress slightly hitting
my thighs. I put on my open toe, high heeled, black, strappy
shoes that were made out of a sort of silk ribbon type of
material that tied up my legs. I left the house around 6:25
after checking myself out from head to toe, front to back in
the downstairs floor length mirror.

Before I knew it I was entering the Lincoln Tunnel.
Looking at the clock on my digital dashboard, it was 6:45
and there was no traffic. I could be there within 10 minutes.
I was cruising through the tunnel listening to Teena Marie's
new song, "I'm Still In Love." Teena Marie is a bad girl.
It's amazing how her voice is still just as strong and crystal
clear as it was from my childhood days. I'm talking about
at the very least 20 years ago she was blazing the airwaves
with "Square Biz" and "Fire and Desire" with Rick James.
Only true Teena Marie fans would remember her sultry
tunes like "Out on a Limb" and "If I were a Bell."

Listening to the words in her new song I pulled up to

Jezebel's and noticed Leon's black big body Benz sitting in front. How in the hell was he lucky enough to find a park right in front? I was swollen because I had to park almost a block away and although my shoes were cute and sexy they were not made for walking. It was 7:05 when I finally made it to the doorway of the restaurant. I strolled up to the hostess table trying to camouflage the aching I was feeling in my feet.

"Hello my name is Kiyah Simmons I have a 7 o'clock reservation for this evening. I'm expecting a guest as well, has he arrived yet?"

As the hostess, a very slim, but attractive African American young lady in her mid-twenties, was checking her list. I scanned the restaurant to see if I could spot Leon. But I didn't see him. The restaurant wasn't that - big so where in the world was he?

"Yes, Ms. Simmons. Your guest arrived *on time* at 7 o'clock sharp. If you would please come with me, I will lead you to your table." Missy spoke with a hint of sarcasm. I'm thinking, '*Now I know this bony chick ain't trying to come for me. What does she mean articulating the fact that he was on time? Was she trying to point out that I was 10 minutes late? Trust me, she don't want to catch it from me tonight. I will take out every ache these shoes are causing me right now on her little puny behind.*' We reached the table where Leon sat waiting for me, which was behind the grand piano that sat in the middle of the restaurant to the right. That's probably why I could not spot him from the hostess table. The hostess who later identified herself as

Amy said, "Here you go Ms. Simmons" and then she turned to Leon "Sir your guest has *finally* arrived. If *you* should need anything, just let me know. Again, my name is Amy. Otherwise your waiter will be over momentarily," she stated as she proceeded to walk away. Now I'm wandering what is her problem with all of this 'he arrived *on time*' and 'your guest has *finally* arrived' stuff? Maybe she had her sights on Leon or something. I don't know - but I am not the one.'

Immediately, I tapped her as she was making her way pass me. "Excuse me, Amy. I'd like a tall glass of water with lemon while I wait for the waiter, thank you." Then I added, "I must say that the HELP here is very hospitable. Listen very careful, please sweety. Make sure that the bartender puts quite a few lemons in my water please." Before she could answer I cut her off with, "thank you so very much. You are a dear." Furiously she walked off. Leon stood up, pulled out my chair and helped me to sit.

He whispered in my ear, "Kiyah you are too much and you look incredible tonight."

"Thank you."

I sat down admiring him in his deep grey two piece walking suit made out of fine linen. He opted to utilize the shirt as a jacket instead. He had on a black silk tank top underneath, with the shirt completely unbuttoned, draping around the tank top. He wore a black alligator skin belt with shoes to match. He was looking and smelling good - real good. As he sat there, the dimness of the flickering lights in Jezebel's just made his caramel skin so illuminating from this angle. If the truth be told, I was ready to leave this place. Just looking at him, made a sista ready to get busy.

"So Kiyah, what's been going on?" Leon questioned.

"Nothing, what's been going on with you?"

"You know - the same ole, same ole. However, I've been thinking of you and I am so very pleased that you found it in your heart to have dinner with me tonight, because there are a few things that I would like to straighten out with you once and for all." Leon stared straight into my eyes.

"Go ahead, Leon. Knock yourself out, but let me warn you, I have zero tolerance for anymore of your, 'I was just trying to protect your feelings' lies," I said with my eyebrows raised.

"Kiyah sweetheart, I have no intentions on lying to you ever again."

As I was about to respond to Leon, when Ms. Ann, I mean Amy came over with my water. That low-budget chick had the nerve to slam my water down without saying one word to me. It will be a cold day in hell before I wet my tongue with anything she serves. Leon grabbed my hand, as I was motioning to get up and snatch girlfriend, to see just what her problem was.

"Baby calm down, let me handle this."

"Did you see what she just did? That thing has a problem

and I refuse to be treated like this in a place that I am patronizing." I said now furious.

"I know, I know, sweetie. Calm down. I'm going to handle it, just calm down." Leon motioned for one of the waiters to come over.

"Yes sir, how can I help you?" a young Indian man that spoke very good English said to Leon as he approached our table.

"Can you have Amy to come over please? I would like to speak with her," Leon said calmly.

"Sure. No problem."

Within minutes Amy was sashaying over to our table with her sunshine girl grin.

"Yes, what can I do for you?" she said with all teeth standing in front of Leon and her back to me.

"As a matter of fact, you can explain your abrupt conduct in serving my companion a glass of water approximately 2 minutes ago."

"I'm sorry. I'm not sure what you are referring to."

"A few minutes ago you came over and slammed down the glass of water with lemon that my guest requested," Leon persisted.

"I'm not sure what you want from me sir. Would she like another glass of water? ....or did something spill?" she inquired with her hands on her hip.

"No, as a matter of fact, I think an apology would be appropriate. She's a little offended and I wouldn't want anything to hinder that beautiful smile from lighting up this place."

I couldn't help but blush.

With a funky attitude Amy turned to me and said, "I apologize if my conduct was in any way inappropriate. Please have dessert with your entrée on us."

"Thank you," I said as she quickly left. "I mean to you Leon, thank you for handling that for me." I touched his hand as it rested on the table.

"Sweetheart you don't have to thank me. I just want to make you happy."

"Leon, how can you do that and you have a wife?"

"She's not an issue. I'm not really with her. Look we have people that depend on us staying together as a symbolic foundation of covering for their souls. I'm the pastor and she's the first lady - that's the extent of our relationship. Kiyah, I love you and I can sit here right now and tell you that I have no desire for her. I fell out of love with her well over 15 years ago. If you won't be with me, it will eventually be someone else. I am not even attracted to her, but I do care about her. Leaving her, would crush her to death, not to mention our children. I owe them that much if nothing else but to save their mother from embarrassment and excruciating pain." Leon paused as the waiter came over to take our orders. I decided on the baked chicken with greens and wild rice. Leon had the same.

Once the waiter left, he continued, "Kiyah you don't have to worry. You won't be slighted in the least. You can have all of the luxuries that my wife has and more. Trust me. If you say that you will give me another chance, I will make sure that you never regret it." Leon sounded so convincing.

"Leon, it's not going to be that easy. You hurt me. I trusted you, especially as a man of God. I can't take anymore lies." Before I could finish, Leon interrupted me.

"I promise baby, no more untruths - believe me. I never wanted to lie to you Kiyah. I was afraid of loosing you, that's all. Look, can we start all over? This time with my hands up and my mouth wide open." Leon lifted both hands in the air, (as if confessing) making me laugh.

"We'll see. You know….I don't have the kids this weekend, so I'm not in a rush to get home tonight," I said in a very alluring tone.

"Just what are you saying, Kiyah? 'Cause you know I'm no sucker. If you deal me some cards, I'm going to play them and there will be no misdeals." Leon always could think so wittily on his feet.

"I'm saying that I don't have the kids this weekend, so I'm totally free," I answered back, but really inside I was saying *'Look nigga I'm backed up, so let's eat so that we can get out of here and get this party started.'*

"Okay, we can have the waiter wrap our food up and go somewhere quiet where we can eat and relax.…'cause that dress is barely containing my friends over there, and you know that I can't resist those beautiful attributes of yours." A little sweat broke out on his forehead, as he was referring to my breasts.

*'Uh, huh here we go.'*

"You know Leon, some of the girls are going to Cancun for Memorial Day weekend and I…." was all I could say before Leon interjected.

"Say no more. I'll have Paul make your reservations on Monday. He'll make sure you're staying at one of the finest hotels out there. He'll arrange for a rental car for you and I'll make sure that you have more than enough spending money," Leon said without so much as taking one breath. He wanted some bad. I could tell that right now I could get him to purchase a Ferrari if he thought he had to, in order to get me into bed tonight.

"Leon, are you sure? I was just mentioning it to you. You don't have to feel obligated to do that for me," I said looking innocent, but check it; if he thought that he was going to get into *these* thongs tonight, he betta had known what time it was.

"I want to do something special for you, so why don't we just call it a peace offering? After all that I put you through emotionally - it's the least I could do."

"Leon are you sure?....'cause," before I could continue he interrupted again.

"Kiyah, please don't mention it. It's nothing, really." To seal the agreement, Leon grabbed my hand from across the table.. At that moment I really felt assured that he was cool with everything or anything I should say.

"Okay, Leon. Thank you so much. Now let's eat some of our food while it's hot, then we can have the rest wrapped for later."

"Whatever, you say, sweetheart." Leon smiled with confidence.

The food came. I ate maybe half the food on my plate, it was simply delicious. Leon just dabbed at his food until he noticed that I was finished with mine, before calling for the waiter to come and wrap our food up.

While the waiter was wrapping up the food, Leon excused himself to go to the men's room. I noticed that it was taking him more than a few minutes to return, so I turned around to look in the direction of the men's room to see if he was on his way back to our table yet. But when I looked - not only was he out of the bathroom, he was having a heated conversation with Ms. Amy. This was a bit much....Why in the hell was he having a private conversation with her? At first I started to get up and march right over to where they were and give everybody in the place a full fledged performance. As I examined the look on Leon's face, I decided to wait and give him a chance to explain. Not to mention the fact that Leon looked like he didn't want to even entertain her conversation. Leon had a calm, almost amused look on his face, but Amy was all frowned up and shaking her head from side to side. When he saw me looking his way, he told Ms. Ann to excuse him. Before I could question him good, Leon started explaining as he approached the table.

"Sweetheart, are you ready to go? I'm ready to get out of this place. It's really a shame, the food is wonderful, but the staff is a little less than desirable. Did you see that young lady, the hostess over there expressing her dissatisfaction with the way I had demanded her to apologize to you for her conduct?"

Uuh huh, I sort of figured that, 'cause that chick had nerve.

"Get out of here Leon. You've got to be kidding me!"

"I wish I was, but yes. She was actually trying to give me a piece of her mind. If I wasn't such a gentleman I would've embarrassed her. But enough of that foolishness, are you ready beautiful?"

Leon offered me his hand, assisting me up from my seat. As I was rising (with my body facing Leon) I gently turned my head around on the way up. I could feel someone looking at

me – only to discover it was Amy looking intensely at us. So
intense that she had a delayed reaction. It took her more than
30 seconds to turn and walk away. What was her problem? I
know I put her in her place and all, but really - it wasn't that
serious.

We left the restaurant quickly after Leon paid the bill. We
got in his car, which was right in front of the restaurant.
As he was closing the car door after letting me in, I swore
I saw Ms. Amy peering through the curtains at us. Why
in the world would she be that concerned with us? First
confronting Leon and then watching us through the window:
I know I had given her a little fever in the restaurant but not
enough for her to be watching us. Maybe she was looking
for someone. I decided to not pay it any mind and not even
mention it to Leon.

After I had gotten into my car, Leon followed me to an
overnight parking garage in Mid-town Manhattan, where I
left my car. He took care of everything, then we hopped in
his car. Dhortly thereafter we were pulling up in front of the
Marriott Marquis.

After Leon secured our room, he asked me would I like to
have a drink in the lounge first before heading upstairs.
*Now look at him, a minister, trying to get me intoxicated
so that his calling would be sure tonight. But little does he
know I had already made up my mind to give him some from
the time I accepted his invitation for dinner yesterday.*

"No, Leon. I really would like to go on upstairs, take a
shower, and get comfortable. Do you mind going out to find

me something to put on?" That's the good thing about New York, it never sleeps. You can purchase a whole outfit after midnight.

"Of course, sweetheart. I'll have someone from the concierge take care of that right away. You're a size ten, right?" All of his attentiveness was turning me on something terrible.

"Yes, but if he's shopping with some of the more elite designers like, Tahari or Dana Buckman, I would need a size 8," I answered. (*If this isn't a hint or what.*)

I'm going to work them pockets this time for sure.

"Alright, I got it. Take this key. We're on the 10th floor. I'll be right up. Don't take that shower without me," Leon said while grabbing me around my waist to kiss me slightly on the cheek.

Once Leon gave me the food and the key, I headed towards the elevator to go upstairs to our room.

When I reached the room, which was number 1,000. I could tell from the outside that it was a suite, because it was situated at the end of the hallway all by itself.

As I entered the room, there was a living room; to the immediate left was a bathroom and then further up to the left was a formal dining room. Off to the right of the dining room was a small kitchen. Then I opened the double doors opposite of the living room area; inside was the master suite complimented with a private full bath. I put the food on the dining room table and decided to check my cell phone for messages. More than once I felt it vibrate at dinner with Leon. I didn't answer. Wow, I had 8 missed calls. I dialed my voicemail and listened to the 5 new messages. The first was from Michael asking if I wanted to go horseback riding with him and Kyasia on tomorrow morning. He must be crazy. I planned on riding in the morning but only on top of Leon. The next three messages were also from Michael - asking and demanding that I call him back. All I could here from the 3<sup>rd</sup> message before he got cut off was, "Where are you and why aren't you answering your phone?" This was amusing. Let him wonder. After all, I had to do it for 15 years while he was wandering the streets pushing up on anything and everything in tight jeans. The fifth message was from Miles, "Hey Kye, what's up? I was just calling so that Kaseem could tell you good night. So, when you get this message holla at ya boy." Aaah, Miles is so sweet. All of a sudden I felt guilty being here with Leon and I really had to call back. After all - Kaseem wanted to tell me good night. I'm thinking, *What if Leon comes in and Miles hears his voice. Think quick Kiyah*

I grabbed the ice bucket, snatched up my cell phone and pocketbook and then pulled the chain from the door outside between the door and the door panel, so that Leon could get in if he comes before I come back. Once I got to the vending room, I dialed Miles house. It must have only rung once when Miles quickly picked up.

"Yo'," Miles said in his own way of saying hello.

"Hey, Dimples. What's up? I got your message."

"What's going on Kye? Yeah, your little man wanted to say good night to his mommy, but he's knocked out now." Miles said in a low tone.

"Oh, Okay. Give him a kiss for me," I said peeking out the door to see if I saw Leon heading towards the room yet. I couldn't tell from this angle though.

"You got it. I'll give you a call tomorrow afternoon."

"Alright, I will talk with you then and thanks for everything."

"No doubt, it's all good."

"Good night Miles," I got ready to hang up the phone.

"That's what's up. I'll talk to you tomorrow."

Quickly I got the ice, two bottled waters and headed back towards the room.

I realized that Leon hadn't come upstairs yet - this was a relief. So I put the water in the fridge, placed the ice bucket on the table, plopped myself down in one of the dining room chairs and finally took off those sinful shoes. I sat there for maybe twenty minutes massaging my feet before I decided to turn the television on. After sitting there not even paying attention to what was happening on the screen for another 15 to 20 minutes, I decided enough is enough. I went into the bathroom of the master suite and started the water running for my shower. I like for the bathroom to be steamed up when I get in. I went back out into the living room area to get the Bath and Body sweet pea shower gel and splash out of my purse. *'Oh yes, this was pre-meditated murder. Leon was going to be dead on arrival.'*

I returned to the bathroom and placed my toiletries on the edge of the tub. I started to take off my clothes, when I felt a hand grab me softly around my waist.

"Let me help you with that," Leon said assisting me with pulling my skirt down; at the same time he was gently kissing my hips, then my thighs; pulling my skirt all the way down to the floor and allowing me to lift my feet one at a time out of the pile of material that had formed on the floor.

"Oooh Baby, I want you so bad, I've missed you sooo much, I can't wait" Leon said while lifting up my top and gently pulling down my bra so that my breasts were exposed. Immediately through the bulge in his pants I could tell that he had arrived. I'm thinking, *'oh, Lord I'm not sure that I want to do this.'* I climbed into the shower with him stripping quickly and following me in. I began lathering up my body with shower gel. Leon was helping me as he began to rub suds gently over my arms and then my breasts. I knew I was finished when he took my breast one at a time into his mouth and started caressing them with his tongue. It was a done deal. I will just have to repent later.

"Oh my God, Kiyah! You smell so good, I can't wait. Umph, umph, umph! Damn girl."

Did he forget that he was a minister? Well if that's the case, so will I. Before I knew it, I was in arresting position with my hands clutching the shower wall and my legs spread wide apart. Leon held my breasts from behind as he penetrated me with thunderous strokes that felt like heaven as his manhood constantly made pleasurable circles of rhythm inside me. It was tight at first, but it felt so darn good after I relaxed my muscles. Oh yes! I knew where to run too when I needed some relief. This man was like Alka-Seltzer plop, plop, fizz, fizz and ooh 'aah relief.' I haven't had any in almost six months and this man was an awesome lover. We must have went at it for over thirty minutes before I said let's go into the bedroom. My hair was a mess from all of the steam in the bathroom. I couldn't buy a curl right now. Thank God for those Dominicans, 'cause they're everywhere. I planned to get me a doobie in the morning. Once we were in the bedroom, Leon wanted to continue where he left off. I don't know where he gets his stamina from, but thank God for his Momma and Daddy.

"Baby, are you okay?" Leon said as he held me close in his arms.

"Yes,"

"That was unbelievable. Now you know I can't let you get away from me again. You know that, don't you?" Leon whispered.

"I'm going to take my shower now while you stay here and relax." I tried to get up and move away from that subject.

"Stay here with me, just a little while longer. I want to discuss some things with you."

"Leon, please. I don't want to make any plans or arrangements. Let's just take it one day at a time." I was annoyed.

"Baby, what's wrong? I know that I haven't been completely honest with you in the past, but I'm more than willing to make that up to you now."

"There are certain things in life that you just can't make up for. You can try and try - but you hurt me Leon. You cut me deeply....At some point there was a healing, but even when wounds heal – they leave a scar. And that scar will always remind me of the pain.

"Kiyah, I'm sorry sweetheart. I didn't realize I hurt you so badly. I'm just anxious to make things right between us again. I love you and I need to know that you're mine again. I thought that since I treated you like the queen you are - that my being married inflicted only minimal damage. However, now I can clearly see that you must have really loved me too. 'Cause you could have accepted the fact that I had a wife and continued to see me knowing that I was going to fulfill your every heart's desire. Wow! You really just wanted me. That's why I don't hesitate to give you everything Kiyah. Trust me - I'm no fool. I can see gold diggers a mile away. Don't get me wrong; your fingers are shining, but you've got genuine feelings with yours," Leon said sitting up and hugging me from behind.

"Leon, I don't want to discuss this right now. Let's just take it one day at a time and see what happens," I got up to go into the bathroom.

Ooooh, this shower was feeling good. As I lathered up, I thought about how good Leon could make my body feel. My body tingled from the sensations. After I finished my shower and sprayed my body with my "Sweet Pea" Body Splash, I wrapped a towel around me and walked into the room with Leon.

Oh, my God! Leon had the bed full of Victoria Secrets. It must have been at least 6 or 7 boxes of lingerie. Then there was a garment bag from Saks containing a black Tahari tailored made two-piece pants suit. It was sharp! The jacket was balero style and the pants were flared at the bottom with slits on each side. I decided to put on a pink see-through lace two-piece shorts and tank top from Victoria Secrets.

"Leon, where in the world, did you get all of this stuff from at 9 o'clock at night?"

"It was only a little past 8 when we got here, and there's a mall right down the block. Do you like everything? I picked you up a velour sweat suit from Lady Foot Locker. It's in the bag on the table out there with your sneakers and flip-flops. You wear a size 8 in shoes, correct."

"Yes, but this is too much. Why did you buy all of these things?" I asked looking at him in amazement.

"It's nothing baby. Besides, I know those shoes were killing your feet. I wanted to get you some sneakers so you could be comfortable while we tour the city tomorrow and do some shopping on 5<sup>th</sup> Avenue." Leon said laughing.

"Funny, real funny. Anyway, thanks but I think you have already done enough shopping for one weekend." I snuggled up against him. By now he had put on his boxer shorts and was drinking some ice water.

"I know you'll change your mind when you see the Louis Vuitton store with 3 floors and across the street is the Fendi store and across from there is the Escada store," he said with excitement.

"Well…. maybe a little more shopping won't hurt nobody," I said leaning my head on his shoulder.

Leon kissed my forehead and after sitting there for about 10 minutes, he got up and took his shower. Afterwards we decided to order room service. I wanted some hot food. I ordered jumbo shrimp scampi and Leon had the seared blackened salmon. We ate and watched half a movie. Before we knew it the sun was waking us up bright and early on Saturday morning.

# Chapter 4
*Caught Up*

Instead of going to get my hair done, I decided to pull it neatly back into a ponytail. Thank God, it was lengthy and still straight from the perm I got at Sybil's in Vauxhall, NJ on last week. Once I put a little make-up on and earrings, I could earn a pass with my hair undone. Leon asked me to order breakfast while he took a quick shower. I ordered us both Continental breakfasts'.

By the time Leon was out the shower, I had my things laid across the bed. The pink trimmed in white, Roca Wear very light weight velour sweat suit was cute. The G-Unit sneakers matched perfectly.

"Leon, I ordered breakfast. It should be here in a moment. I'm going to hop in the shower in the meantime. Okay?" Leon's phone was ringing; so he just shook his head indicating that he heard me, as he answered his phone.

"Hello," he spoke into the phone. "No, I'm out of town.... Oh, I thought I mentioned that to you. I apologize. I'll give you a call later when I get back." Leon was speaking in a soft tone. I imagine that must be his wife.

I don't know why, but I was standing there paralyzed with my hands on my hip. *'How dare he advertise his marriage in front of me like that? At least when he was lying about it, he had enough respect to hide it.'*

I couldn't say anything. I had no right to be angry. I knew he had a wife. Yet, I desperately wanted him to validate my position in his life. It's funny, how he could buy me all these expensive things and still make me feel cheap. As I stood there, he turned around puzzled as to why I was still standing there and not in the shower.

"Kiyah, sweetheart what's wrong? Why haven't you taken your shower yet? We need to have breakfast and get out of here in a timely fashion so that you can have ample time to spend some of my money today." Leon bragged with a grin on his face.

"Leon, don't start with me." I knew he was trying to divert me from his phone call. At that moment I didn't care about any shopping. I didn't want him talking or apologizing to any other woman, besides me. I couldn't take him explaining his whereabouts to anybody else except me. I was still in love with the stupid jerk. I never stopped.

Before Leon could respond, there was a knock on the door. I figured it must have been room service. As Leon walked out of the room with a puzzled look on his face, I decided to get in the shower and try to calm down my emotions.

Oooh, it was like heaven. I stood under the warm water, letting it flow downwards. I felt the need to shampoo my hair in hopes of clearing my thoughts. Rinsing my hair, the old Temptations' classic came to mind, "I Wish It Would Rain." That's what I wanted it to do. I wanted it to rain. Rain so heavily that it would wash away all my bad decisions, my disappointments, my mistakes and most of all my heartache and pain. I needed time to rewind so I could do some things differently in my life. *'Why am I here?'* I could fool myself if I wanted to, but I knew there was no way I was going to settle for just being his mistress. The best thing to do was leave now, while I still could. *'But I still loved him and I didn't want to be without him.'*

As I cried silently, the running water blended with my tears. I guess this was a shadow of things to come, when indulging in an ungodly relationship. You can only hope for at best *bitter sweet* moments of pleasure and happiness. Moments later, I re-lathered. I rinsed myself for the final time, I felt a lot better. I had made up my mind to enjoy the day.

I exited the bathroom with my towel wrapped around me, to find Leon standing there with one of the hotel robes. He must have gotten out of the closet. I jumped from his unexpected presence clinching my towel to keep it from falling down.

"Listen Sweetheart, I know that you're a little agitated from my phone conversation earlier." Right then as Leon was talking, my mind was speaking again....*You got that right. Agitated is an understatement. He better be glad that he had gotten it last night 'cause right about now his little phone conversation had made me want to turn off the oven and pad-lock it up.*

"But I want to assure you that I love you, I need you and I want to be with only you," Leon said as he put the robe around my shoulders helping me to put it on. In between his words he was kissing my neck and cheek.

"Leon, if that's true, then stop answering your phone and give me your undivided attention; at least during breakfast." I turned my face around just enough to allow him to kiss my cheek while holding me from behind.

"Alright, darling I promise I'll do that just for you" Leon walked me over to the sliding glass doors that led to the balcony of our room. He had taken our breakfast out there. *What a romantic thought.* We had a wonderful and pleasant conversation as we ate breakfast overlooking the magnificent and busy city of Manhattan.

Leon's phone continued to vibrate during breakfast. Every now and then he would look down just to see who it was, but he never answered.

Finally, I was satisfied and could no longer force myself to eat anymore of the delicious fresh tropical fruit that was served with my breakfast which consisted of: french toast, turkey sausage and scrambled eggs and cheese. Leon sat back glaring at me and bragged

"Kiyah, God has been good to me. I'm a successful minister. I have more money than I will ever spend in my lifetime, I am able to leave my children with some security, but today Kiyah I can feel the sun is shining especially for me and you know why I know this to be true?" Leon asked as he grabbed my hand from across the table.

"Why?" I answered mesmerized.

"Because....I'm here with you. This is a blessing Kiyah."
Leon stood up and came over to my side of the table. *I have
to admit, I've seen a lot of game in my life, but his is the
smoothest of the smooth.*

"Leon that is so sweet."

"It's the truth baby. I am so pleased and especially happy.
We've had a wonderful evening on last night that cannot be
compared to any other and today will be more of the same.
So why don't you hurry up and get dressed, so that we can
do a little shopping like I promised," Leon said helping me
up out of my seat.

A *little* shopping?...Huh! Ain't nothing little about the way I
shop. Put me on 5th Avenue in the middle of Manhattan with
a good credit card and it's a guarantee the stock market will
go up.

I put on the sweat suit (compliments of Leon), which fit me
like a hand in glove. It clung to every curve and I decided to
wear the jacket, without a shirt underneath, zipping it up just
enough to leave a hint of cleavage showing. Now I know I
need prayer.

I was not about to be caught dead in the heart of New
York City without giving a little bit of fever to the streets.
Luckily I was able to cuff the pants to make them look
more like Capri's. This look allowed me to wear my black
high heeled strappy sandals that tied up my legs instead
of those sneakers that matched. I'm really not one for
sneakers anyway. I knew those shoes would be killing me

73

within 2.5 seconds of strutting around on 5<sup>th</sup> Avenue, but I was willing to endure the pain for the sake of *DIVA-ISM*. Hey, somebody's got to do it. My black on black Gucci bag completed the look. As for my hair, I pulled it up into a ponytail with my black scrunchie using my fingers to fluff my hair up. I was half way to cute. As I looked into the mirror I could see how my baby hair had formed curls around my edges. I put a little powder on my face and gloss on my lips. I was all the way there. You know.... to cute. Now I was ready.

"Baby you look good," Leon kissed me on the cheek.

"Thanks,"

"Are you ready sweetheart?" Leon asked as he opened the door. Umm I could tell that he wanted to come back here to get his compensation for today's shopping trip, because he was ready to leave without taking our belongings. Oh well, it's all good.

"Yes," I said as I made my way pass him and out the door.

The car was waiting out front for us when we reached the lobby. Leon was must have called ahead for it.

Once inside the car Leon asked, "Where would you like to go first honey?"

"Leon, I don't know, where-ever is fine. You know we really don't have to do any shopping. We can just tour the city"

"Come on baby, what woman wouldn't enjoy a day of shopping in the fashion capital of the world?" Leon said patting my leg as he was turned into the traffic.

"Leon you are so sweet. You know everyday that I've spent with you since we met has been more like a fantasy," I said looking at Leon and oooh he looked so handsome.

"That's exactly how I want you to feel. Baby, I want to make all of your dreams come true. I can do that for you, Kiyah. Trust me." Leon said and then continued.
"Why don't we check out that Escada store on 5th Avenue? I brought you their perfume, but I heard they make clothes, shoes and all sorts of things as well. Why don't we check them out first?....What do you think?" Leon asked glancing over at me.

"Sounds good to me," I answered.

Within twenty minutes we pulled up to 5th Avenue in front of the Escada Store. Across the street was the Fendi Store and down the street maybe a block away were the Gucci Store and Louis Vuitton. Already just from looking at the stores from the outside, my stomach got queasy. This was too much for one woman to intake all at the same time. There were doormen at the door to open the doors for you as we entered the store. This was unbelievable. As I went in, the first thing that I noticed was the clothes. Leon must have noticed because he suggested that we go over and take a look. I tried on several outfits selected for me by the store fashion coordinator. Once in the dressing room

I peeked at the prices. Wow! ....$225 for a skirt, $310 for the jacket and $115 for the tank top. This outfit was sharp and perfect for church. 'Look at me I just got finished sleeping with somebody's pastor and now I'm worrying about looking appropriate for going to church. We've got it mixed up now-a-days. We should be more concerned with acting appropriately in order to one day become part of God's Church. Now I know I need deliverance; anytime I can preach to myself and still don't take heed to what I know is right. Lord you know, that's why you wrote in your Word that the love of money is the root to all evil and the O'Jay's hit it close to home when they penned the song, "For the Love of Money," it will make you kill your own brother; but it gets bigger than that especially when you don't realize that you're killing yourself. Compromising your self-worth, money or materials shouldn't be able to obtain or define your self-worth. It should be so high, that it will be considered unattainable. My mother always used to tell her girls, "A man should always think that he doesn't deserve you. It shows his admiration for the woman you are, but as soon as you allow him to give you gifts in exchange for your body, he will never feel that he doesn't deserve you, instead he'll feel like he paid for every single second of your time and every inch of your body. Not only that, these men nowadays got the nerve to think you owe them something. Y'all betta watch yourselves." I could here mommy's voice just as plain as if she was standing here right now. *'Mom I'm sorry for letting you down, your not here anymore for me to run to for advice or counseling. I know you're up there in heaven looking down on me, balling me out right now. I promise mommy, I'm going to get it together real soon.'* Hearing Leon outside of the dressing room snapped me out of my deep thoughts. I walked out.

"Kiyah, I really like that sweetheart. It looks great on you," I was turning around in the mirrors right outside the dressing room. Then he turned to the young lady that was helping us and said, "We'll take that."

And that was the key phrase for the entire day, "We'll take that"

Leon was on the phone most of the time that we were shopping. He was mostly talking about speaking engagements and church business.

We went upstairs and got a bag and shoes to match my outfit. "We'll take that" was all Leon would say. Now it became a phrase to pacify me while he excused himself to answer his phone.

Louis Vuitton was our next stop, and just like Escada, basically everything that I admired, Leon would purchase.

When we left out of Louis Vuitton, instead of going directly over to the Fendi store, we took our packages to the car first. Walking to the car, I turned and looked at Leon. He was so handsome in his gray on gray velour sweat suit, a white Titan's fitted cap, with some fresh white Air Force sneakers. Not to mention his immaculate jewelry: a long white gold chain with diamonds separating each link, a matching bracelet on his right wrist, (normally he wore a Rolex watch on his left wrist) but today he sported a white gold Movado with a stream of diamonds outlining the band on both sides, a diamond pinky ring on his left hand. On his right ring finger he wore another diamond ring mixed with green jades set in white gold. Leon was a man of perfection. As I was watching him from the side, he was turning me on. Steve Harvey couldn't get a better outline on his (hair) cut. Everything was perfect about this man. Deep inside I knew being with him wasn't right, but how could I resist?

Every now and then, Leon would turn to me and smile, while he was still on the phone. Finally I stopped walking. I wanted him to get off the phone and this made for a good excuse to get some relief from the burning these shoes were giving to my feet.

"What's wrong?" Leon turned to me and asked.

"I want you to get off the phone" I answered.

Leon smiled and spoke into his ear piece. "Look man of God, I'll give you a call later to finish this discussion, I need to handle something right now. You know a minister's work is always in demand," he said laughing as he hung up the phone.

I was heated. What did he mean he had SOMETHING to handle? I'm not something. My name is Kiyah. Now I know what Destiny's Child meant when they wrote the lyrics, *say my name, say my name if you ain't running game say my darn name.*' Not to mention that he ended the conversation insinuating that he was engaged in ministering work. I'm just tired, but I'm not going to black out on him right now, not while he's looking so tasty, and especially not before we pay Ms. Fendi a visit.

"Okay, sweetheart I'm off the phone," Leon said flashing that delicious smile of his, showing off his perfectly polished white teeth.

"Finally….Leon, you know this is ridiculous. You have been on the phone practically the whole time we have been shopping today."

"I know baby. I apologize, but my schedule is very hectic lately. You know how important my career is to me. I'm trying to accommodate the two most important things in my life all at the same time. I know I have things I need to attend to at the office, but I want to spend some time and spoil you today. I promise not to take another call today. Just let me place a call into my office to give my secretary instructions for the rest of the afternoon. Then I promise you can have my attention along with the rest of me. Okay?"

That was sweet of Leon to say and just like that I couldn't be mad anymore. He knew just what to say to make my heart melt.

"Okay," I said as Leon pulled me close to him and kissed me gently on my neck.

As Leon was speaking to his office, we continued to make our way to the car. Once we reached the car, Leon put the bags in the trunk and closed it. He grabbed my waist, held me close and kissed me passionately. *'Oh my God did he smell fresh.'* I just wanted to stay right there in his arms. I thought that this feeling was never going to end.

Suddenly, Leon stopped holding me. When I looked up at him to see why - he had a paralyzed look on his face as he was staring over my shoulder.

Immediately I turned around and looked in the direction he was staring in and I saw a short, stocky refined woman walking angrily towards us.

"Leon is something wrong?" I asked, but he didn't answer.

As the woman got closer I asked him again, "Leon is something wrong? Who is that?"

By this time she was almost to us.

"Kiyah get in the car," Leon softly said to me as he was pushing me gently towards the car door.

"What do you mean GET IN THE CAR? LEON WHAT'S GOING ON, WHO IS THAT?" I was resisting Leon's efforts to get me into his car.

"I AM HIS WIFE, YOU SCRUMPET!" she blasted as she walked directly up on us.

## Chapter 5
*Here We Go Again*

I couldn't believe what was happening and better than that, I couldn't believe how Leon's wife looked. Not that she was a bad looking woman; on the contrary she was quite attractive - very fair-skinned, with soft features. However, she just didn't appear to be his type. But who am I to determine that? After all, she is his wife. The reason why I figured her not to be his type is because she wasn't flashy like him but instead sort of matronly. It's funny, because you can tell that she had money by the quality of clothing she was wearing, yet it was all in poor taste.

She wore ordinary red dress pants (which only amplified her chubby frame) and to add insult to injury she paired it up with a soft pink sweater and a red scarf around her neck. Absolutely no imagination what so ever and how creative of her to find some of those Naturalizer shoes in pink.

"Your wife, Leon?" was all I could say before he pushed me into the car.

"LEON, I AM SICK AND TIRED OF YOUR MESS! FIRST THING SUNDAY MORNING I AM GOING TO GIVE THE CHURCH MY RESIGNATION…..YOU ARE A LIAR, A CHEAT AND TO TOP THINGS OFF, YOU PICK THE HEART OF NEW YORK CITY TO PARADE YOUR WHORE AROUND."

'Who in the hell does she think she's calling a whore, I'm

not a whore.'

"Look Tonya, I know how this must look, but why don't we meet at the house and talk about this civilly," Leon said smoothly.

"Meet at the house? nigga ain't no more house, 'cause your ass is out as of today. Now let your little streetwalker out of MY car so that I can whoop her behind." She was trying to open the car door from the outside. Leon kept pulling her hand from off the car.

"Tonya cut this out! You're not going to fight anyone. You're a first lady, a woman of God, you can't be out in pub....," was all Leon could say before his wife slapped the skin tone off of his face.

"How dare you, try to patronize me with the very thing that has caused me to accept your bullshit over and over and over again." She paused for a moment, looked at me through the window and then turned her venom on me. "And you, YOU low-budget, cock-sucking, trifling whore....GET OUT OF MY CAR, before I bust this darn window and pull you out," she said while pounding on the window.

'Oh NO, darling. I NEVER sucked his cock and low-budget....NOT! Ask your man?' I was thinking as this so called evangelist was out here in the middle of FRONT STREET calling me everything but a child of God. Because that's what I am, a child of God, who is need of His help. Even though right now I am double dead wrong but I'm still a child of God. He said He'll never leave me nor forsake me.

Even when I stumble just like I've done over and over again. Even right now as I'm stumbling, God is still in standing position ready to move on my behalf. I needed to pray 'cause, the way this *thing* is pounding on this window, she might be liable to turn the whole entire car over.'

'Lord I know I'm wrong, but I need your help right now. God if you get me out of this situation I will NEVER let you down again. Jesus please, 'cause you know that I can't take this woman calling me all these names, (even if they are true.) I just can't take it, Lord. She doesn't know me like that. I'm from Newark (the Bricks) and I will bust her down.' I couldn't help but get heated as I was praying thinking about; all of the names, Leon's wife was calling me. I didn't appreciate it. She oughta be directing her anger at him not me.

First Lady, or not – it was time to beat the b---- down! She called me out of my name one too many times. *Scrumpet?! Streetwalker?!* I'll streetwalk all over her a--! Granted, I know I'm wrong because he is her husband but if She-Wolf don't calm down, I'm goin' *have* to bring it to her.

"Get out the car TRICK" she yelled through the window.

"TRICK?! What the f---? That's it, that's it!" *Ooops! Religion: temporarily absent.* Time to whoop that ass! I squirmed over to the other side of the car to get out.

As I was getting out, I saw Leon chasing after his wife as she was racing around to the side of the car, that I was now getting out of.

Leon barely caught her before she could get to my door.

"Tonya, cut this out. She doesn't have anything to do with this. I can't allow you to hurt this young lady. This is all, my fault not hers," Leon said while restraining his wife's hands. I know he didn't want to experience anymore of her blows.

"I don't believe you have the brazen nerve to sit up here and defend your whore in front of me. Nigga, I'm going to ruin you. You'll never preach another sermon in your life." As Tonya blurted out the words, it seemed as though she regretted it. She clutched her mouth as if she had committed an unforgivable sin.

"WHAT?! You'll do what? You're not going to do anything…."

'Who was this person? Because the smooth, debonair, classy man I had just spent the night with, had went straight STREET!

Leon grabbed his wife and threw her up against his or hers (*whoever's*) car and *now* she was the one paralyzed.

"I'm not going to let you or anybody else *rob* me of what I have worked my entire life for. You sit your fat ass up in that 1.5 million dollar home that *I* pay for and don't even bother to workout or diet to get in shape for me. You spend over $50,000 dollars a year on clothes that don't even look good on you. You get honored twice a year at our church, just because you're *my* wife. You can buy anything you want, when you want to. You don't have to move off your fat ass to work for it. You know why you can do all of that?..... because of *me*! MY GIFT! *My* preaching has provided us with a lifestyle that you would *never* experience, if I hadn't been so skillful at what I do." Leon shoved her up against the car. I know he forgot that I was there for a minute, because when he collected himself, he instantly regretted his actions and looked extremely uncomfortable. This was the side of him that he didn't want me to see.

'*Thank you Jesus*,' was all I could think, 'cause I could have woke up dead this morning. I had spent the night with Michael Meyer's distant cousin and didn't know it.

Leon finally calmed down and let her off the car. She was pitiful, crying with her head hung down. He had his back turned to her looking amiss into traffic. I was stunned, I couldn't believe this. I didn't know what to say or do.

After an awkward period of silence, I decided to just walk away.

I didn't get too far, maybe a block and a half away, before I felt the presence of someone behind me. It was Leon and thank God he decided to catch up to me because besides everything that had just transpired between him, his wife and myself; the only thing I could think about was the merchandise from Escada and Louis Vuitton waiting for me in the trunk of Leon's car. If it wasn't for any dignity at all, I would have asked him for my bags before walking away.

"Kiyah! Sweetheart! Please wait."

"Leon, what are you doing?....go back there and take care of YOUR WIFE," I snarled as I continued to walk.

"Come on Kiyah. Please hear me out. I need you to just stop and listen....I'm not going to chase you around Manhattan, not on foot anyway." Leon tried to catch his breath while keeping up with my pace. My shoes were already killing my feet, so I decided to stop.

"WHAT?! What could you possibly tell me *this time* Leon?"

"Look, I can't just stand here and talk to you like this.... please, let me get rid of her, then we can talk."

As Leon was pleading his case, his wife had the *audacity* to walk up on us. I thought I was gifted with foolishness but she wins that award. This man isn't worth a dime and she's running behind him, even after he has embarrassed her in front of another woman, namely me. I may be backsliding, yet I'm struggling to hold onto my salvation. She's a first lady and he's a pastor, yet blatant hypocrites struggling to hold onto their status, not even considering a soul like me. Wow, I can't imagine how God is going to deal with them. I was standing there, hurt and destroyed in the company of so-called representatives of God and neither one of them *ever* stopped and considered my spiritual need.

She marched towards us like she was performing for the Macy's Thanksgiving Day Parade. Face all turned up, like she was too ready to handle her business. I wouldn't dare run behind him. She should at least wait until she gets him home to give him strife.

But she couldn't rationalize, not now. She was too emotionally distraught and couldn't think sensibly. So, she just invested more stock into being a *Fool on Display*.

"Leon, I can't take anymore of this. I mean it. First of all, you told me that you needed to make sure she had cab fair."

"CAB FAIR!" I looked at Leon like he was crazy, as his wife continued to rant and rave.

She continued, directing her attention to Leon as if she hadn't heard a word I said.

"So, why all of this chit - chat? See, Leon? I can tell that you want to continue playing these games, but I'm serious. I'm no longer going to deal with it. I really mean it this time, Leon. You're going to have to choose now! It's either: me, the church and our children or these women you continue to run around with. You're going to tell me right now in front of her," she demanded with her hands on her hips.

"Tonya, you know that I would never put anything or anyone before my ministry, so why are you doing this? Kiyah and I are just friends; at first it was innocent only about the ministry and I'll admit that I might have went a little beyond those boundaries....but I promise you that nothing ever happened between us.... I just got extremely upset and I apologize for my behavior, but it drives me crazy when my own *wife*, tries to use my ministry against me. How could you? It hurts Tonya....really it does. I preach in season and out of season, in town and across the globe - just to provide you and our children with all of life's pleasures," Leon is full of sh-- . That son of bi--- is such a liar, I ought to crack him across his forehead right now. Lord have mercy 'cause I couldn't believe what I was hearing. This nigga ain't sh--, excuse my French, but he might as well start selling tickets 'cause his a-- is definitely qualified to star on Broadway right now.

But check this out - I ain't about to say one single word, *not until I get my stuff.* I was shocked and extremely hurt, but that's quite alright, because I just learned a very valuable lesson. The only difference between a rich nigga and a broke nigga - is the money. No matter what, they will still have major game. I know now, the money will only determine where you'll sit watching the game. Either way, if your chillin' in his Benz, or his hoopty.....trust and understand that you are, *(now don't miss this)* you will still get played - whether you want to believe it or not.

"Okay Leon that sounds good and everything, but I SAW YOU standing over there all hugged up with this TRAMP and you really expect me to believe this crap you're telling me now.....Huh? I don't think so," Tonya said still questioning him.

Now I'm contemplating.
I grew up in the church all my life and I have a great deal of respect for Pastors and First Ladies. 'Oh! But this chick is

about to *catch it*, she's got one more time for the word tramp to fall from her lips and I'm going to have to give her the business.'

At this point I'm silently praying to myself.
*'Lord, what am I doing here? This is utterly crazy. This so called preacher was all up in me last night acting like he couldn't live without me, took me on a whirlwind shopping spree and constantly proclaimed his love for me. Now here I am standing here in front of him and his wife and he's acting as if he didn't know me at all. Father you've got to find me a way of escape right now, because if I stay here much longer, I'm going to commit a crime.'*

"Come on Tonya do we have to go through all of this right here and now?  This is ridiculous, Jesus!.... if you must know Kiyah is going through a difficult time right now," (*Listen at him using the Lord's name in vain but hey why not he preaches in vain so why not use His name in vain?.... I can see right now that Leon preaches for a lifestyle and not for the winning of souls, so it's all in vain anyway. He has and cares about all of this position stuff in the church and doesn't realize that there are positions reserved in hell for people like him. What am I talking about? If I don't hurry up and get my act straight, I'll be his co-passenger.*) While I was thinking Leon was continuing with his lies.

"Kiyah is in the midst of a separation from her husband and I was consoling her,"

WHAT IN THE HELL?! No he didn't! I stood there ready to slap some truth into his lying mouth. My lips were shaking at this point and I started to feel myself getting emotional. This wasn't something I wanted to do in front of them, nor was it a behavior I was accustomed to exemplifying in public, but my anger was driving me to tears.

Leon grabbed his wife's hands and leading her towards her car. This was a wise choice on his part, 'cause I know he could tell that I was about to let loose.

"Now Tonya, honey, can we discuss this at home? Look what you've made me do. In order for me to convince you of my integrity I had to violate a minister's oath. I had to compromise Kiyah's confidence and disclose her private information, in order to calm you down. I am anointed and appointed by God to do this Work. I don't like to, but I MUST DO IT. I am a minister for the Most High God. He never said it was going to be easy Tonya and when you married me, it wasn't going to be easy for you either. Now please let me walk you to the truck, so that I can make sure this young lady gets home safely and I assure you I will be home to discuss today's incident thoroughly with you. I promise that I will be there within an hour. Is that okay?" Her truck was the blue Eddie Bauer Expedition that he used to drive me all over town with 6 months ago.

As he was walking away, I was standing there and men passing by were trying to "Holla," Actually, one guy didn't look that bad, as a matter of fact he was kinda cute and neatly dressed. He had on Pepe Jean shorts, a white wife beater and some fresh Air Force One's and really nice iced out jewelry, but hey this is New York, who knows if it is real or not? I was too mad to examine him close enough to tell the difference. He wasn't that tall; approximately 6 feet even and dark brown skinned with a winning smile. Ummn…. what a chocolate delight? Not to mention the body on this Mrs. Field's chocolate chip cookie. He was buffed, just in the arms and back; not too much, but just the way I like it. I don't go for the body building steroid looking types. *'Yes Lord! He was perfect.'* As he approached I noticed he had brown sugar colored bow-legs looking so sexy.

"What's up Ma? Why you looking so mad? Smile you're too pretty to be all frowned up,"

Wow, I didn't even realize that my emotions were showing up on my face for the world to see. I needed to take control of myself and hit a Jay Zee on this situation – *'brush this dirt off my shoulders.'* Leon was that dirt, why did I jump in bed with him so fast? I guess that's what makes him think that he could just play me the hell out (like he just did) 'cause I already showed him that I'm more than willing to be played. Now here this fine brotha was kicking game, trying to get my number by telling me that I was pretty. I wasn't in the mood and trust me - he didn't want it, not from me anyway. I don't feel pretty right now. I wanted to tell him that I'm not pretty - I'm just *pretty stupid;* stupid, for trusting a man that has already proven to be untrustworthy. I was stupid for selling myself cheap, willing to comprise my dignity and self-worth for a few bags of top of the line labels. I wanted to tell him to run like hell, 'cause the only men I'm attracted to are worthless. So if you are about anything and God forbid if you're anywhere near decent - I'm not the one, 'cause at this point I wouldn't even know how to act.

Inside I was crying and overwhelmed 'cause the reality of the whole situation had set in. I thought that I was getting the goods from him, materialistically anyway, but all he did was *rob me* of my self worth in exchange for Louis Vuitton and Escada, (a hell of an exchange for my virtues and morals.) He didn't even have to put the gun to my head - I did it myself the day I started to allow myself to be defined by what I wear and what I drive. Although these thoughts were running through my head it was consoling to know that this fine specimen of a man thought I was pretty. I must not look too tore up, he's cute and still standing here. Suddenly I felt a teeny bit better.

I didn't respond but only blushed by his comment, which opened the doors for him to continue.

"My name is Shyne. What's your name? I'm not going to ask how you're doing 'cause I can see that your fine," he said flirtatiously.

I could see Leon from where I was standing and this was a grand opportunity to give him fever. 'Cause I know when he turns around and sees me talking to this scrumptious looking treat, he is going to be HEATED!

"My name is Kiyah."

"Okay, Kiyah. Wow, what a nice name. It's nice to meet you. I would really like to get to know you better, so do you think that I can get your number so that I can give you a call?" Bingo! Do I know them or what?

"It ain't that easy playa. I don't just give my number out."

"Well, how am I going to get in touch with you?" he said softly.

Dag, I can tell that he was a sweetie right off the back.

"I don't know sweetheart, why don't you give me your number and I will call you?" I said not giving in.

"Naw, it's like that Kiyah? Don't do me like that. You're seriously not going to give me your number?" he continued to question. Just then I saw Leon coming towards us and I got instantly nervous. Why? I don't know 'cause after today I don't owe him anything.

Anyway, I was forced to give my number to Shyne, in order to get him ghost before Leon got to us.

"Okay Shyne, if you can remember my number you can have it. I'm going to say it quickly and then I must ask you to leave, because the man approaching us is meeting me for a very important business discussion and I don't want to be rude."

"No problem, I understand. I'm ready when you are and trust me I won't forget your number Kiyah," he said now smiling, he was definitely a cutey and oooh so sweet, I can just tell.

"My number is 973-555-1234. I hope you got it Shyne,

'cause I'm not going to repeat myself."

"I got it gorgeous and I'm out; handle your handle....you take care of yourself," he said as he began to walk away. As he turned to the side I could tell that he had a fresh, clean hair cut under his fitted cap 'cause his sideburns were perfectly outlined. I love a clean cut man and this is one of the things that my radar always picks up. If a man keeps a clean cut, he is normally clean, well groomed and smooth.

But wait, his side profile also revealed his long baby doll eye lashes. He was a doll, I mean a real doll. I wish I would have gotten his number because now I was noticing things about him that most certainly motivated me to give him a call.

As Shyne disappeared into the crowd of New Yorkers, Leon made his way over to me.

"Kiyah, sweetheart; I'm so glad you held your peace just now in front of Tonya. I know that it was difficult for you, but I appreciate your decorum. You are truly a remarkable young lady; any other woman would have...." Leon was all ready to start his bull crap, when I rudely interrupted him.

"Leon, Shut the Hell Up!"

## Chapter 6
*Liar, Liar, Pants on Fire*

And that's just what he did while we made our way to his vehicle. I don't know whether he was shocked by my response or maybe his lips was exhausted from all of the lying he had been doing, but he didn't say another word while we walked back to his car.

When we reached the car I asked him to pop the trunk so that I could get my things.
Don't think I wasn't. I pulled my bags out of the trunk and proceeded to walk away. Leon was finished, whether he knew it or not - to hell with his old a--. His hair was beginning to recede anyway. That's why he's always sporting a cap. I don't have to put up with his crap. It's funny how a person you once thought was so attractive can suddenly loose their appeal when you finally identify how ugly they are inside.

"Kiyah, come on; cut this out. You still have to at least get your things from the hotel room," he pleaded, trying to follow me as I was walking away.

"Now WAIT A MINUTE, Leon. I'm not going with you any…." I stopped mid-way, before I said something that would eliminate some ample opportunity.

See sometimes I have to catch myself. 'Cause this was definitely an option worth considering. I did have 3 outfits, some G-UNIT sneakers and some flip flops still back at that hotel room. So now, I must go back to the hotel with him. I don't want to, but I have to, if for nothing else but for the sake of the High Fashion Society. It would be against the principle of Fashion itself to let some good expensive well designed clothes go to waste.

Once I reconsidered, I stopped and informed Leon that I would allow him to take me to get my things, all the while warning him that there was no chance in hell that he was going to get any action in the process. I was totally through with him this time. He just disgusted me.

I didn't talk to him the entire way to the hotel and half way there he stopped trying.

Once we got to the hotel, I asked him to go up and get my things alone while I waited in the car. Mainly because I didn't trust him, and secondly, I had a few phone calls to make. Angrily he got out the car and proceeded to go get our things solo.

While Leon was gone, I called Miles to check on Kaseem. Miles didn't answer his home phone. I checked my watch; it was 3 in the afternoon. Wow, time had flew Miles and Kaseem had to be leaving football practice by now. I tried Miles on his cell, it rang maybe twice before he answered.

"What's Up Kye," Miles voice always seemed to comfort me.

"Hey Miles, I was calling to find out what time you wanted me to pick up Kaseem?'

"It's not that serious Kye. Whenever, or I could just drop him off later. What's your schedule like for today?" Miles said, always extending himself.

"I'll be home within an hour and after that it's a wrap. I'm taking it down." I was anxious just at the thought of getting some rest.

"Okay. Why so tired, Kye? I was going to ask if you felt up to a movie and dinner tonight with Little Miles, Kaseem and myself," Miles stated inquisitively.
Now I was feeling guilty. I could see that Miles was serious about trying to take our friendship to another level, but I'm just so afraid. Miles is a good guy and I don't want to hurt his feelings, 'cause I love him. I am so confused right now and I owe him at the very least more than that.

"Gosh, I'm sorry Miles. I would love too, but I'm so exhausted. I wouldn't be any company for you guys, maybe another time."

"Whatever. Yo', listen Kye; I'ma holla atchu when I'm on my way with Kaseem. Let me get off this phone and get at these boys," Miles seemed disappointed.

"Okay, Miles. Thanks for everything."

"No problem, I'll talk to you later." Click.

I don't know what's wrong with me. Miles is great, but I just can't see it right now.

After Miles hung up I dialed Kyasia's cell phone. She answered right away.

"Hey, Ma….why haven't you called me? Where were you at 12 o'clock last night 'cause me and Daddy rode past our house and your car wasn't there?"

"Slow down, Kyasia….I didn't call you because I was tied up all day. My car wasn't there last night because I was out with a few friends, honey. But from now on don't you make it your business to check up on me sweetheart. That's not your job. I'm grown and I can stay out because I'm capable of making responsible choices. I'm the one that's supposed to check up on you.
 Now, how's everything going with you today?" I said almost breaking out into a sweat. This child doesn't miss a beat. Every now and then I have to remind her that I'm the mother and she's the daughter.

"Maaaa, I'm doing alright, but I'm ready to come home. I don't want to hurt daddy's feelings but I feel more comfortable at home with my own things." She sounded just like my little angel. I can't believe how much she has grown. Seems like only yesterday; I was just giving birth to her, and now she's almost 13 with a mind of her own.

"Okay, Kyasia. I'll be home in an hour, so ask your father to drop you off sometime after that."

"Okay, Mommy. I'll see you when I get to the house."

"Love you."

"I love you too mom," Kyasia hung up the phone.

As I was hanging up with Kyasia, I was thinking what am I doing here? I'm a church baby. I was baptized and filled with the Holy Spirit at the age of six and preaching by the time I was thirteen. Now look at me. I wouldn't want my daughter to grow up and make the decisions I've made. My mother is probably turning over in her grave right now. *Lord have mercy!* If the members of my father's church ever found out. It would be a major scandal. The pastor's daughter is running around with a married man. Oh yes, I can here those *Holier than Jesus Himself Church Folk* right now labeling me as a home wrecker….the harlot that brought down the ministry of a thriving young black minister. Yet amazingly enough, these are the very ones that are supposed to be there for me to run to for prayer and support. I was shivering from the thoughts of being exposed when I saw Leon coming through the sliding glass doors that led in and out of the hotel. At the same exact time, my phone was ringing. The screen read, "Queen Bee." Uh oh, Lord knows this just put the icing on the cake. Queen Bee was my oldest sister and since my mom had passed, she now took on that role in our lives and for some reason at times I think she wallows in the authority aspect of things.

"Hello,"

"Kiyah, where are you? I haven't heard from you since Thursday evening," Queen Bee questioned, sounding concerned.

"I'm in New York. Just got finish doing a little shopping, but I'm on my way home now. Is everything alright?" I questioned.

"Oh you're in New York shopping and didn't tell nobody? That's okay. Where's Kaseem and Kyasia?"

"Kaseem's with Miles. He took him to football practice for me and Kyasia's with her father. He took her horseback riding, so I thought this was a great time for me to get out and get a breather." I wasn't lying, I just wasn't telling the whole truth. Deep inside I knew that Queen detected something was wrong. She just chose not to address it right now. Leon was busy putting our things in his trunk. I really wanted to get off the phone with Queen before he got back in the car, but it didn't work out that way 'cause Queen was still talking 99 miles per hour. Leon got in the car and didn't say anything.

"Oh okay, how long will it take you to get back 'cause they had to rush Benita to the hospital. Ever Ready is on her way to pick me up, so we can meet Wali down at the emergency room." Ever Ready is my middle sister (the one that will fight in a heartbeat) and Wali was my oldest brother. He was meek and mild tempered with a good heart. He and Benita had been married for over 20 years. I know he must be extremely worried right now. I really needed to be there to support him.

"WHAT! What happened?"

"Kiyah, calm down that's why I needed to make sure the kids weren't with you when I told you, 'cause I know how emotional you can get with your dramatic self. Benita lost consciousness and stopped breathing. Wali found her on the bathroom floor. He immediately called the paramedics and started CPR. By the time they reached the house, Wali had revived her but her breathing was still shallow. So they rushed her to the hospital by ambulance. I've already contacted the rest of the family and they're on their way. You be careful traveling back; take your time and don't worry God is still on the throne. This family has taken a lot of punches but we've managed to stay in the match. Kiyah? Kiyah? Are you there?" Queen yelled.

"I'm here Queen. I'll be there as soon as I can," I said through tears.

"Okay, just be careful. You know we'll be at Beth Israel."

"Of course, I'll be there."

Of course I knew just where they would be. Beth Israel hospital was the hospital that I was born in, the hospital my mother died in and the hospital that I gave birth to both of my children in. This was the place that my entire family trusted to handle all of their medical needs ever since I could remember.

But ever since my mother died there, I couldn't even ride pass there without my heart aching. I remember picking my mother up from one of her physical therapy sessions in the rear of the hospital. They had given her physical therapy to help her get used to having one leg after the affects of diabetes had claimed her left leg. Anyway, we were in the back of the hospital and one of Cotton Funeral Home's hearses pulled up in the back and over to a drive up port across from us. Two orderlies rolled out a body with a burgundy velvet sheet over it. I looked at my mom with fear in my eyes. Just the thought of death always scared me, and with my mother's health declining, it terrified me the most. The thought of an end coming to the person that had given me my start was devastatingly scary. My mom reached her hand out to me and said, "We must pray for that person's family 'cause one day I'm going to have to go that route."

"But mom, I don't want you to die. I don't want to live, if you die," I said crying at the thought of it.

"Aww Kiyah, it's okay. I've lost one leg; they're talking about taking the other one. I don't want to be just a shell of a woman. I want to go to my Father's house where I will instantly be made whole," my mother said with a tender smile on her face.

"Mommy, you've got eight children; that's sixteen legs. We'll be your legs mommy; just don't ever give up ma. We need you," I pleaded through burning tears.

"I know, baby. I continue to fight because I love you kids so much and I would never want to leave all of you, but I'm tired and I'm tired of fighting. It's in God's hand now. But don't worry 'cause He's not going to take me until all of my children can take it. His Word says that, 'the Lord will not put more on you than you can bear.' That's when it's going to happen for you, Kiyah. You're going to soar like an eagle my darling Kiyah, but only once I'm gone. I've got to go in order for your destiny to be released. My departure is going to be your entrance into greatness. You've been so dependant on my strength all of your life. When I'm gone, that's when you're gonna find your own strength and you'll finally see just how strong you are when I'm no longer here to pick up the pieces. If a person doesn't like mess, then they are going to have to one day learn, how to pick up after themselves. You're beautiful, smart, good-hearted and a lovely young lady. Don't settle Kiyah....don't settle," That's all mommy said and just rested her eyes listening to the spirituals I had playing in my car during the ride back to her house.

As I was sitting in Leon's car with tears streaming down my face, I remembered that day which had to be at least 5 years ago. Mommy passed approximately a year and another amputation after that day. I never thought about that day since, but today it stood out in my memory and believe it or not, I needed my mother right now. I was scared for Benita, I was ashamed of my actions and I was as confused as a blind mouse in a maze. Yet God had sent me a memory (that when it was reality I didn't realize) that would be able to comfort me 5 years later. I needed my mother so bad, but now I realized that I never lost her. I will carry her in my backpack of memories for the rest of my life. Just like a rolodex I can find a memory of wisdom from my mom to suit every occasion in my life. When she carried me in her stomach we shared the same heartbeat. Now that hers has stopped, my heart has picked up her beat.

"Thank you Jesus!" I yelled through my tears. I didn't care if Leon thought I was crazy or not. God had just blessed my soul and I didn't deserve it so, I had to thank Him. Nobody knows but God just how much my heart aches for my mother each and everyday of my life. If I could just hear her voice one more time....if only I could pick up the phone and call her like I had done at least a dozen times a day when she was alive. But I can't - 'cause she's gone.

*"Lord, I know that I'm not supposed to question you but why? Why did you have to take the very best friend I ever had in this entire world?"* I whispered between my tears.

"Kiyah, are you alright?" Leon said as he patted my leg. I didn't say a word but just continued to pray.

'Jesus, thank you God for the memories, thank you Jesus for watching over my kids and Lord thank you for giving me the spirit of fear, 'cause if it weren't for fear of going to jail. Lord I would stab this nigga next to me right now. I'm so tired of men, Lord. I need you to send me someone that you can love me through. I no longer want the kind of love that a man can give. Lord I need Your kind of love, yet through a man. Send me one of Your vessels. Bless Benita right now God. I know I'm not in a position to make any requests but Lord please not for me, but for Benita. Make her whole again Lord." As I was praying silently, Leon persisted with his questions.

"Is everything okay sweetheart? I heard you on the phone. Did something happen?"

"I need to get home as soon as possible. How far are we from my car?" I asked in almost a whisper.

"Don't worry. We'll be there within 10 minutes, but if you want I can drive you over to Jersey. You seem too upset to drive. I can bring you back to pick up your car later," Leon persisted.

"No, that's okay. I just want to get to my car. I will be fine."

"Okay, we'll be there in a few minutes," Leon said rubbing my knee to comfort me.

I didn't want him to touch me. He disgusted me with his pretentious self.

My mind was too pre-occupied to tell Leon's behind off for the stunt he pulled this afternoon. So I decided to just keep quiet and pray until we reached the parking lot where my car was parked.

Once we finally arrived, Leon jumped out and took care of the bill. Then he climbed back in the car with me while waiting for them to drive my car up.

"Kiyah, this has been quite a day and I'm so sorry, sweetheart. I know you need to get home, but I was hoping that when things settle for you at home, maybe we can get together late this evening to just discuss things. I know that this may sound crazy to you Kiyah, but in light of everything that's happened today, I still would like to continue this relationship." Leon pleaded while holding my hand.

I was numb; I didn't care about love, commitment and loyalty any longer. Just listening to him made me understand just what the women my husband sold dreams too were falling for. This same B.S., they will continue with their lies in an effort to keep those panties conveniently down. But what the hell, I don't give a darn anymore. I'm finished searching for that fairytale marriage that comes with the house and the picket fence. It's never going to happen anyway. The only thing out of that scenario that can be realistically obtained is the house, so now why shouldn't I make mine a mansion?

## Chapter 7
### *Spinning*

I couldn't stand Leon right now, but I was still very much in love with his money, his ways and definitely his style of life. Deep down inside I was madly in love with the Leon I first met; the one who swept me off my feet, and took me on a whirlwind romance for 6 months. After everything that has happened today, he has the *uninhibited nerve* of asking to continue to see me.

Maybe I would see Leon again, why not but trust me it's going to cost him every time.

I never told Leon that I had considered seeing him again before I left. I couldn't possibly do that. It would be going against the ultimate code of Diva-ism. A true diva could never give in so easily. She must always keep in line with her status by always, (I mean always) making a person sweat a little.

I wasn't through the Lincoln Tunnel good before Leon was calling me.

"Hello," I answered softly.

"Hey, sweetheart….are you sure your okay?"

"Yes, I'm fine. Why are you calling me? You should be preparing your lies, getting them in sequential order before facing your wife." I couldn't help myself. I was bitter.

"Come on Kiyah, don't be like that. How do you think I can do the things for you that I do? It's my ministry that affords me that ability and unfortunately she is tied to the success of my ministry. If she exposes my infidelity then I would be at risk of loosing everything I have. As much as you benefit from that Kiyah, I'm sure you wouldn't want me to give that up. Besides, I was just on the phone with Paul and I gave him instructions for planning your trip to Cancun for Memorial Day weekend."

Now this was motivation, I felt my anger starting to ease instantly. Maybe I could have that mansion sooner than I thought. Why not?

"Thanks Leon, but I don't know if I could accept that from you. I don't want you to feel that everything is okay between us because it isn't. I just need time to sort through some things."

"Okay sweetheart, you do that and Cancun will be a great place to start….I will call you later to see how your doing. Just let me know if you need anything and I will be praying that everything is okay with your family,"

I'm thinking. *'Oh heck no, I don't need you praying for me and my family. Your prayers aren't going pass the ceiling of your car. I might as well sign Benita's death certificate if we're dependant on your prayers.* If it's one thing I knew ever since I could remember and that is **only** the prayers of the righteous availed much...Right now I needed one of Mother Wagner's prayers to get us out of this mess. Mother

Wagner was one of the old prayer warriors from my home church Ecclesiastics Church of Christ on Beacon Street in Newark. She was the one my mother always called upon to pray our family through some rough times.'

"Thanks, Leon but everything will be fine. I'll talk with you later." I said preparing to hang up.

"Okay, don't hesitate to call me for anything, ANYTHING," Leon said with sincerity.

Even though I knew that the only place he had genuine sincerity was resting below his belt, I remained polite. *I had to* because sure as my name is Kiyah, I will be taking that trip to Cancun with the quickness.

"I will, talk to you later," I said hanging up the phone.

By this time I was already through the Lincoln Tunnel and maybe 10 to 15 minutes from the hospital. While driving I called Miles and explained to him the situation and asked if he could keep Kaseem until I left the hospital. He agreed with no hesitation. That's my Miles, always there for me. I called Kyasia and told her to have her father drop her off over Queen Bee's house where my other nieces and nephews were. I could have let Miles drop Kaseem off at Queen's as well, but I didn't want to take a chance on him and Michael running into each other, especially since Michael doesn't like the idea of Kaseem being around another man.

By the time I got the kids situation settled I was already on Lyons Avenue looking for a parking spot near the emergency room of Newark Beth Israel hospital. As I road pass the entrance to the emergency room, I noticed about 6 of my family vehicles occupying most of the spaces right out front. My heart start beating fast when I saw that Elder and Sister Howard's car was there as well. I knew something was wrong, Elder and Sister Howard have been there for my family through thick and then. When my mom's health was declining, Sister Howard was right by her side until the very end. Elder Howard was a shoulder and rock of strength for my father through out that whole ordeal. Even now after mommy has passed on, they have remained loyal to that friendship. Whenever tragedy strikes this family, they are the two people that are always right there to lend us strength and support.

I finally found a parking space on Osborne Terrace which was a complete city block away from the entrance of the emergency room. My cell phone rang just as I was entering the hospital, but I didn't recognize the number. My mind was on Benita right now, so the phone call would have to wait. Within minutes, I made my way through the automatic doors that led to the reception and waiting area of the emergency room. I could see through the glass windows Elder and Sister Howard standing there talking softly to Daddy. My Dad, Bishop Simmons, who is the coolest preacher I have ever known, was standing there rubbing his head, looking perplexed. To Daddy's left was my brother Jared standing next to Ever Ready who was sitting, and from the tore up look on her face I knew it wasn't good. Benita's sisters were both wiping away tears sitting across from Ever Ready and my brother Shot Gun was pacing back and forth biting his lip like he just wanted to hurt somebody. Once inside, instantly my eye zoomed over to my twin cousins Charletta and Charlene, standing in the corner near the vending machines.

Before I could get inside good, Ever Ready jumped up and ran to me screaming, "Kiyah, **Benita**, **Benita**," was all she could say through tears before she collapsed.

Thank God Jared and Shot Gun was right there to catch her. At this point I was dropping tears myself and so was everybody else in the emergency room. Some of the church members were there also. I didn't notice them at first.

I went over to Daddy, who was looking a little thin lately. I guess my mom's death was starting to take an effect on him.

"Hey, Dad....are you okay?" I asked rubbing his left shoulder.

"Sure, I'm fine. Go on in there and check on your brother and sister." Daddy was trying to hide that he was worried.

That's my dad always trying to stay strong for the rest of us. He has always been a pillar of strength, even when mommy had passed. He never cried at her funeral, just requested that the casket, remain open for the entire service. I guess he wanted that moment to last forever. It was the last time he would ever see her face again - the woman that he had been married to for over 45 years and had bore him eight children. I knew that must have been the hardest pill for him to swallow: demanding that the casket remain open. Wow.... maybe that was his way of grieving. Through all the rough

times in our lives, this man has always been the solution.
I know that it was only by the grace of God. I remember
when I was pregnant with Kyasia and wanting to run behind
Michael all the time. He took me to New York while I
didn't know at the time that Michael was going to pick up
drugs to later sell for more money in Jersey. But anyway
he got caught on the way back because the cops found the
drugs in his car and locked both of us up. I'll never forget
the look of disappointment on my dad's face when he came
to bail me out the next day in court. I know he must have
felt shamed, but he never downed me or made me feel bad.
He just stood before the judge and pleaded for my release
and the judge let me go with no bail. Daddy left Michael's
behind right in there and me with my crazy self instead of
being glad that I was out, I wouldn't let my father rest until
he helped with Michael's bail. Now I know this must have
tore him up inside. He had worked hard, provided for us
eight kids, sent me to college and there I was throwing my
life away on a no good bum and pregnant to boot.

"Who?....Ever Ready and Shot Gun?" I asked.

"No, Kiyah. Wali and Queen, they're in there with Benita
and I'm worried about Queen. She's trying to be strong
for Wali, when she's barely able to take much herself."
He paused for a second and then Daddy just flipped and
continued, "We need to get in there and pray and see what
the Lord has to say." Daddy spoke with cracks in his voice.

"Oh, okay. What room are they in?" I hesitated. I don't
know why, but I was scared to go in there and see Benita. I
was afraid. I could smell the scent of death all around me.

It was lurking in the air and I felt totally paralyzed.

"They're in the first room on the left," Shot Gun stated looking so upset.

I walked to the back and asked the guard to let me in. With no problem, he let me in and I nervously opened the doors to Benita's room.

"JESUS!" Was all I could say when I saw Benita's body laying up there so limp. They had a tube down her throat and a confusion of more tubes hooked all over her. Wali was sitting next to the bed holding her hand and Queen stood next to him rubbing his shoulders comfortingly.

"Kiyah, the doctor said that there isn't much more they can do....Oh Kiyah...." Queen couldn't help but break down.

"No, not again.... not Benita....," I had to catch myself. Although I was tore up inside, I had to think of Wali, I didn't want to make him feel worse. He was sitting there just as calm, I know he must be breaking apart inside. But just like my dad, he wouldn't dare show it.

"Queen, Daddy wants you and Wali to come on out, so that they can come in and pray with Benita," I said through whimpers.

"Y'all go on out, I'm not going anywhere," Wali stated softly, yet firmly.

"Are you going to be okay, Wa?" Queen asked squeezing

his other hand.

"Yeah, let Benita's sisters come in with Daddy," Wali said solemnly.

Queen and I walked out holding hands. Holding her cheek with her other hand, Queen turned to me and said, "Kiyah, I don't think Benita's going to make it."

"Don't say that Queen, she's going to pull through." I squeezed her hand tightly.

Daddy, Elder Howard and Benita's sisters went in, while we all waited outside in the reception area.

Minutes later, Daddy and Elder Howard came out yelling, "Hallelujah, Glory to God.....HALLELUJAH! There is POWER, Wonder working power in the name of JESUS!.......Kiyah, you can, ......THANK YA!" The Spirit had hit Daddy again as he tried to continue. "Glory! Kiyah, you and Queen can go on home now....God has had His say. Thank you Jesus!" Daddy said with his hands stretched out and a little sweat dripping from his brow.

"You mean Benita is okay?" I asked, but before Daddy could answer, Wali came out and told Ever Ready and Shot Gun that they along with the twins could go in now. But what fell out of his mouth next caused me, (yes, sinful me) to shout out and give God some praise.

With the brightest smile on his face, Wali turned to us and said, "Benita is sitting up and trying to talk!"

"Thank you, Jesus!" Queen and I both said together.

"Kiyah, Queen.... you don't know what this means to me. The doctors say that the cancer has spread throughout her whole body and it's nothing else they could do for her. I've accepted the fact that she was going to have to go with God soon, but her laying up there comatose....Oh, my God! I just wanted to see her beautiful eyes looking at me once again and if I could just hear her voice one more time, I knew that I would hold on to that for the rest of my life. I just wanted another shot at grasping that memory." Wali had a thin line of tears rolling down the side of his face. He didn't even bother to wipe them and amazingly this was the most my brother had talked in months. He was the quiet type, but he was full of emotions right now and if he didn't get them out he was going to burst. I held Wali's hand as Queen had her left arm around his shoulders sitting him down. The twins came over to comfort him as well. A lot of good they were doing 'cause as soon as Charlene saw Wali crying, she started crying.

"It's alright Wali," she whined and her twin Charletta followed suit.

"You'll be okay," Charletta kneeled down and rubbed Wali's knee. My twin cousins, for so long it's always been them and us: Connie's and Eleanor's kids. Our mothers were the closest sisters I've ever seen and they raised their children to be just as close. So it's only natural for them to hurt when one of us was hurting and vice versa.

Anyway, through the tears Wali explained how Daddy and Elder Howard came in the room and started pleading the blood of Jesus! He said the more Daddy and Elder Howard prayed, the more the power of God began to fill that room. Wali demonstrated how Daddy anointed Benita's head and demanded that the spirit of death leave from that room.

"Suddenly, I felt Benita squeezing my hand and then her eyes started flickering...I can't tell you what happened after that because there was a praise in effect.....Thank you God!....going on in Emergency Room #7," Wali's eyes filled with hope and joy.

Whoa! I've never heard Wali talk like this before. Plenty of times he would go up to the altar for prayer or salvation, but I've never heard him give God some praise.

Strange, how God works. He will put you in a situation where you'll have no other choice but to thank Him. Just thinking about what He has done for you, causes a praise to leap out of your belly.

Even with Benita's room number, room # 7 - I didn't even notice. Ironically Daddy always said that's God's favorite number: seven days in a week, seven colors in a rainbow, etc. Thank you, God. Everyone went in to see Benita before leaving. My immediate family stayed with Wali. The doctors told Wali, that he could take Benita home and make her comfortable, it was only a matter of time. They informed him that the hospital would arrange for nursing and hospice care.

After several hours of observation, it was after midnight when they released Benita from the hospital. The doctors couldn't understand her sudden coherency. Earlier, she was totally out of it and now she was gaining strength and even trying to talk. The doctors may not have understood, but I certainly did. God will always have the last say. He loves for someone to count His people out just so that He could step in at the last hour and declare that He is able to deliver you out of a hopeless situation.

So, why can't I grasp my own deliverance? Within myself, I knew it was because I didn't want to be delivered right now. I liked the benefits that came along with the sin I was indulging in, (even understanding that the eternal benefits would be doom.) Yet still, I couldn't help myself. I was banking on the fact that I had ample time to repent and make things right with God. A scary thought came to mind just then....hopefully I'm making the right investment!

## Chapter 8
### *Slippin'*

I had no intentions on going to church that Sunday morning.
Before we left the hospital, we all agreed to take shifts
helping out over at Wali's house. My shift fell right around
morning service. I was understandably irritated when my
cell phone started ringing bright and early around 7:30 in the
morning.

"Hello," I said in a low, sleepy tone.

"Good morning, precious. Today is the day that the Lord
has made. We should rejoice and be glad in it." Leon
sounded like he was rehearsing for his Sunday morning
sermon.

"Leon, I'm still sleep!"

"Oh I apologize, sweetheart. I just wanted to hear your
voice? Can we get together later around nine? I should be
finished with evening service by then."

"I don't know." *(Really I wanted to say **hell no,** but I
thought about that trip to Cancun so I had to at least be
polite'* "Call me around nine and I'll see how I feel. I was up
late last night and didn't get much rest, so let's just see how
I feel by then, okay?"

"Okay, Kiyah....I know you're still upset from yesterday
and I want the opportunity of trying to make things up to

you. But in order to do that sweetheart I really need to see you. You know how I get after ministering to God's people. I need the company of my woman."

"Your woman is YOUR WIFE. Check her schedule, okay?" I just blurted out. I really didn't want to say that, but it just fell out 'cause this nigga really had some nerve, suggesting that I would be willing to put out his flame after he gets all riled up from preaching.

"You know what, Kiyah? I think I need to let you take a few days to calm down. I'm not going to keep tarrying with you much longer. I've never been one to play games and you know that. There are plenty of woman that would love to be in your shoes and wouldn't mind accommodating me with more fruitful conversation. Now LOOK, I provide you with what you want so I expect you to provide me with what I want without hesitation and I won't continue to tolerate you throwing my wife up in my face during every conversation." Oh no he didn't....Dr. Jekyll has exited the building and left Mr. Hyde standing there.

'Think quick, Kiyah. Now calm down and don't react so fast,' I had to control myself. That Project Chick in me was dying to introduce herself to Reverend Ike. Oooh I wanted to tell his a-- off right now, but for the sake of an all expense paid trip to Cancun, I had to hold my **peace** and not give him a **piece** of my mind.

"Leon, you know what? Get a room after service and call me when you get there. I will meet you there. My kids are here with me and I wouldn't want to give them the wrong idea. They are very impressionable at their age." I said this knowing that it would get to him.

"Naw, that's okay sweetheart. Arrange for a sitter on tomorrow night and I'll see you then. I guess I'll just hang out with the fellas for a little while after church and then head home, since I can't be with my woman," he sounded like he wasn't sure how this whole thing had turned around.

After Leon and I hung up the phone, I immediately went back to sleep. Just as my sleep was getting good, my cell phone rang again. This time it was Michael.
"Hello," I said looking at the clock on my nightstand. It was 9:15 in the morning.

"Kiyah, where are you?"

"Excuse me, why are you questioning me?" I said sarcastically.

"I'm sorry Kiyah, I was just wondering if you were on your way to Sunday School, 'cause I was going to drop by and pick the kids up from the church and take them out to IHOP on route 22," he paused just for a slight second and continued, "It would be nice if you would join us, the kids would really, really like that," Michael said with a soft tone. He had a very deep voice and hearing him speak softly, you could definitely tell why the ladies fell for him so fast.

I didn't know what Michael was up to but it wasn't going to work. I was thinking maybe I would go out with them for breakfast if it would do the kids some good. Anyway it

120

meant I didn't have to cook breakfast but most of all - he was finally going to pay for something.

"I don't know Michael. I have to be at Wali's house by 11:30 and you know how crowded IHOP is on Sunday morning."

"Don't worry….I will have you back to the church by eleven. I promise!"

"We're not going to Sunday school this morning, Michael. We had a long night, but I can meet you at IHOP in 45 minutes."

Michael hung up. I jumped out the bed to get the kids up and about. They were really excited when I told them that we were going to have breakfast with their father.

I really didn't know what to wear. I was so used to putting on my church clothes every single Sunday for as long as I could remember. My fashion mind was put off schedule with this whole Benita situation.

Finally I decided to wear Dana Karan, from head to toe: black lacey blouse, boot leg pants and black fur vest. Along with my Via Spiga high-heeled wedged slides and matching bag. I paired my diamond studs with some large diamond hoops from Neiman's (courtesy of Leon). I took my wedding rings off my right hand on purpose. Yeah I still wore my wedding rings, Heck I paid for them, plain and simple. Some people looked at me strange when they notice that I'm still wearing my wedding rings. I guess they thought I was having a problem letting go. SORRY! That's not it; I paid for these rings and his too. Well over $5000 dollars of my hard earned cash. Humph, I'm going to wear these rings until Jesus comes back. Not to mention that I had to reframe from Short Hill's Mall for over six months just to finish paying for the darn things. Anyway I didn't want Michael to see me with them on; he might get the wrong idea. Like I was still trying to hold onto the relationship or something and I most definitely didn't want him to think that!

Before you knew it we were at IHOP. It was perfect timing. Michael was motioning for us over to his table when we came in.

"Wow, I just got seated and you guys came right in. This has got to be a good thing." Michael said as he was hugging and kissing Kyasia and Kaseem.

"Dad....why didn't you take me horseback riding with you and Kyasia?" Kaseem asked right away. Lord these kids don't forget a thing.

"Aww Jr. trust me. I wanted to, but you had football practice. Now that I know your schedule, next time I will plan it for an early Sunday morning, especially for you....if it's alright with your mother?" Michael said looking at me.

"Ooooh Ma, could I....please could I?" Kaseem begged.

"I guess," I said shocked at how Michael had suddenly turned into Mr. Rogers and Bill Cosby all wrapped up in one.

"YES!, now Kyasia, daddy's going to rent the whole joint for me on Sunday," Kaseem said leaning his back and tilted to the side with his arms folded above his chest and his capped hovering over his face. Boy did my son think he was the coolest of the cool.

"Alright Kaseem, that's enough. Sit up straight and don't try and tease your sister,"

"I don't care anyway, I already went horseback riding with Daddy and it isn't that serious," Kyasia responded, looking like she was not beat (in the mood) for Kaseem's little antics.

Wow, I could really tell that she was growing up. Right then Michael and I looked at each other and laughed. Kyasia was too much.

Breakfast was good and Michael didn't start. I must say I was truly surprised, I actually had a good time and the kids were delighted.

It was eleven o'clock when we were standing in IHOP's parking lot and Michael insisted that he keep the kids while I went over to Wali's house. I couldn't believe it, Michael was not the considerate type. My good sense was telling me that he was up to something. But hey, right now it was working out for me.

It was 11:35 a.m. when I walked into Wali's house and

immediately Queen started yelling.

"You're going to be late for your own funeral. I've tried feeding her that nutrition drink through a straw but she doesn't have much of an appetite. Periodically see if you can get her to sip on it. Alright, I have to get to the church; I'm running late 'cause of you. You would think that you could be on time sometime Kiyah. It's a darn shame. You know this a busy day for me," Queen fussed as she was gathering her things to leave.

"I was only 5 minutes late. You act like it was an eternity. Anyway, the kids and I joined their father for breakfast at IHOP and I ran a little behind schedule. But go on to church I'll tell you about it later," I had to laugh, as Queen started putting her things down and grabbing the chair she was in, to sit back down.

"What happened? That bum has the nerve to want to take you'll out to breakfast and isn't paying any child support," Queen said with her hand resting on her waist. Before I could feed into Queen's comment, we both were startled by the noise coming from Benita's hospital bed (provided by hospice).

It was a miracle; Benita was moving her lips and looking in our direction bucking her eyes. At first Queen and I both was staring at her with our mouths wide open in shock because she hadn't moved or opened her eyes since I had been there. We were speechless for one minute and then we just busted out laughing. I really didn't mean to laugh because Benita had gotten so thin and she looked so helpless but she was seriously trying to gain enough strength to get an earful of the gossip that was about to take place.

"No...No...Kiyah I just realized it was you......I wanted to tell ....... You've got to stop running from God.......... God sees your hurt .....your pain but it .......all for .....you to be used by him" Benita said shaking and trying to lift her head up. But she couldn't.

"Benita, lay down.....you need your strength. Please don't try to talk." I motioned for Queen to leave.

"I'm not going nowhere till you tell me what happened between you and Michael today," Queen said firmly.

"Nothing happened. You know? I actually had a good time and so did the kids."

"Oh Lord, I can see you're going to let him wiggle his way right back in your bed and by the way where is my niece and nephew," Queen asked.

"They're with Michael, he offered to watch them while I came over here....I think he's trying to change Queen."

"Lord have mercy, I'm glad God gave you beauty 'cause you sure ain't got no brains. The man is putting on Kiyah, just to get you back. He's probably broke and he figures if he gets back with you all of his finances will be taken care of once again." Queen shook her head in disapproval.

"Don't you take him back.........He's not the one......God has for .......you," Benita barely got out.

"She betta not take him back, 'cause if you do.....I tell you one thing, I'm not going to help you with those kids this time...I love Kyasia and Kaseem to death but I'll be darned if I'm going to let that no good nigga use you and me both," Queen said now grabbing her things to leave.

"I said nothing about taking him back, Queen, what are you talking about?....and Benita," just then I looked over at Benita's bed and she was sound asleep. For a split second I had forgotten all about Benita being sick.

"I know you and I know that snake you were married too. He's slick and you're gullible,"

Queen was upset, she couldn't stand Michael. That's why you have to be careful what you confide in your family with. Because, they will never really forgive anyone that has hurt you; it's all in the name of love though. I know my sister just doesn't want to see me hurt over and over again.

"I'm not thinking about Michael, Queen.... I was thinking about calling that minister that spoke Thursday afternoon for Jared. I think his name was Sean Johnson, he was cute and he even asked me out," I smiled thinking of how handsome Minister Sean Johnson was.

"Now you're talking. I can tell that man was anointed and appointed by God. That's the type of man you should be considering," Queen was walking towards the door. Right when she put her hand on the knob to exit the house she turned around and "He's not married is he?"

"NO, that's the first thing I asked him," I said laughing. Ever since I confided in Queen about Leon being married, she has never let me live it down.

"Oh, okay, 'cause you want to be blessed, so you must strive to do what's pleasing to God. Now I know it isn't your fault if a man lies to you about his marital status, but we have an obligation. We're the pastor's children and we should try to set a good example. Not to mention that God is sitting high and looking low. Everybody stumbles and fall short but we should do our best to not purposely do the wrong thing. Are you understanding what I'm saying Kiyah?"

"Yeah, Queen it's 10 after 12...If you don't hurry your going to miss the morning offering," I said wanting her and her nagging to leave the premises not now but RIGHT NOW! (I guess I still got a sermon this morning)

"Okay I've got to run, don't forget to wash Benita up, change her gown and have her smelling good by 2 p.m. You know the church members will be dropping by to see her after service." Queen could run her mouth 99 miles per hour when she wanted to but right now I was ready to reduce her speed. Lord have mercy she wasn't finished. "Ever Ready will be here at 2:30 to relieve you....and Kiyah, I know you think that I'm always on your back but it's because I love you and I know you've been through a lot this past year and a half. Sometimes when you've been hurt the way you have, well it sort of makes you vulnerable. So I'm just watching your back *girl*, that's why God gave us sisters.... I'm going now and I'll talk to you later," Queen added as she was closing the door.

After Queen had left, I got Benita all straightened out, washed up and ready for company. She never woke up really the whole time I was there. It was only when Ever Ready had came in and I was about to leave that Benita opened her eyes and looked at me while I was leaning over her hospital bed to give her a kiss good-bye.

Her eyes were filled with water as she struggled to get the words out, "I LOVE YOU..... Please.........Remember,"

"I love you too Bee, I'll be back tomorrow and I expect you to be up and about," I said fighting back the tears. I could tell that she was giving up, but I really wanted her to understand that I wasn't giving up hope and I expected the same out of her.

I left Benita's and went straight home. While driving, I called Michael from my cell to let him know that he could drop the kids off to me. But he had already taken them to the movies and it wasn't due to be over for another hour and some change.

The house was noisily quiet. No kids. I was totally bored, it was around 3 o'clock, at least 60 degrees outside and I didn't have anything to do. I decided to microwave some popcorn and catch me a movie on Lifetime and just chill.

45 minutes later, I was just getting into the movie when my cell phone started ringing. As I was reaching for it, I figured it to be Sandy calling to see why she didn't see me in church

today or better yet trying to get the real scoop on Benita's condition.

"Hello,"

"Hello, I'm trying to reach Ms. Kiyah Simmons please," a deep and almost familiar voice replied.

"This is Kiyah....who's calling?" I said curiously.

"This is Minister Sean Johnson. I hope I'm not catching you at a bad time."

"No."

"Good....Well, I was thinking of you today and I was wondering how you were doing so I decided to call and find out. So....how are you?"

"I'm blessed, thank you," I replied right away.

I could tell that he was just as nervous as I was. But eventually we both became more relaxed and we must have talked for about 20 minutes and agreed to make our first official date a shopping trip to the Village on this coming Saturday. Wow, Leon who?

# Chapter 9
## *Easing the Pain*

Monday, Benita was still holding on. Beth Israel's hospice care was there when I arrived around 11:45 that morning. Yes I was late. Wali was holding up well. I hung around with the rest of my family all day and night.

I did manage to run out and meet Leon at Newark Airport's Marriott hotel to get my ticket confirmation and travel arrangements for Cancun. Of course once he got me there, he wanted to do something. I don't know why but I felt obligated to have sex with him. Leon is the type of person you find it hard to say no to. He has this way about him, that makes you want to please him or gain his approval.

We weren't five minutes into it, before I knew that this was going to be one of the worst sexual experiences I ever had, mainly because something had changed. I couldn't put my finger exactly on it, but the magic was definitely gone. Even though it didn't feel right anymore, I pretended like I enjoyed myself and told him that I really had to get back to Wali's house because they didn't know how long Benita was going to hang on. He understood and offered to help. But really there was nothing he could do. I couldn't think of one thing Leon Booker could possibly do to help me out right then, besides staying the hell away from me. It's funny not too long ago I would tingle at the sound of his name but now I just couldn't stomach him anymore.

The rest of the week I spent most of my time between caring

for the kids and helping out over at Benita's. Every time my cell phone rang I was hoping it was Minister Sean, but it was mostly Leon's annoying behind calling constantly, over and over again. I could tell that he sensed that my feelings for him were subsiding. I didn't want to come clean with the fact that I was unsure about a future with him just yet. Not after I had accepted his money and gifts. So, I had to keep reassuring him that everything was okay between us. Even though it really wasn't, 'cause little did he know that he was 2.2 seconds from being replaced.

By Saturday, Benita was still holding on. On my way to meet Minister Sean, I drove by Wali's house to check on them. Walking through the door I could smell death all in the air. Benita looked like she had aged 20 years in just 7 days. She had lost at least 35 pounds and her face was rail thin. Oh my God! I didn't come by on Thursday and Friday because I wanted to get some much needed housework done. I would have never imagined that in two days she could take this sort of turn for the worst. She was wasting away right before our eyes. Just the sight of her made me cry. I was too mad at myself because my make-up was running. Now, I didn't want to go anywhere. I offered to stay, but Wali told me that he was tired of company and he didn't want people seeing Benita like this anymore. He just wanted to be alone for a little while. I decided to let that little 'company' statement pass – I'm not company, I'm family. But he's stressed and not thinking so I went on in the bathroom, wiped my face down with witch hazel and did my make-up completely over again. In five minutes flat my face was beat and I was back looking cute.

I was on my way to Dunkin Donuts on Springfield Avenue in Irvington. That's where Minister Sean and I decided to meet because we both were so familiar with the location.

When I arrived he was already there, looking so handsome. Lord have mercy, he had on sand colored beige cargo pants, a button down shirt with some deep beige shiny leather square toe shoes and a light weight leather blazer that matched his shoes to a tee. Now, what in the world was I going to do with him?

"Kiyah," Minister Sean yelled. As if I didn't see him.

I proceeded to lock my car with the remote and started walking towards him. Once I reached him I went right up to him and gave him a big hug to break the ice.

"Hey, Minister Sean....it's good to see you."

"Likewise, sis....you look great," he said after we hugged.

"I didn't have you waiting long did I?" I asked.

"No, not at all....I must have gotten here minutes before you."

"Good. Look, I'm ready to go. Are you?" I was anxious. He did the wrong thing when he suggested that we go shopping in the Village.

"Of course, my car is right over there." Minister Sean directed me over to a white Mercedes E-class. That was too funny. His car was just like mine, only his was white and mine was black.

"Nice car," I laughed.

After he let me into his car, we talked and laughed all the way to New York. I've never felt so comfortable with someone so quickly.

We were in the Village in a split second or so it seemed because we had such a great time talking. It wasn't long before I realized that we had so much in common.

We had such a great time shopping. Even though we must have gone into over a dozen stores, I only purchased two items, (especially since I was paying for my own things). Sean picked up a shirt out of one store and a belt off the streets. Still we had a great time just comparing items and prices to what they would cost in Jersey. However 99% of the things we saw in the village, you couldn't even get in Jersey.

The day was absolutely wonderful. I was all in. Sean was somebody I definitely wanted to see again. He didn't preach to me. He didn't constantly talk about the bible. He didn't even try to hit on me for sex. He didn't make any sexual comments or nothing like that. He was just refreshing.

We had an early dinner in a café called Maroons in the Village. While we were waiting for our food, Sean asked me, if I would see him again next weekend. I told him that I would be delighted. We got to talking so deeply I even told him somewhat about what I was going through with Leon and Benita. I didn't mention Leon's name because I was sure that Sean either knew or heard of him, since they both were ministers. In return Sean told me about his last relationship with the choir director at his church. He said not only was she directing the choir, but she had a habit of directing other men to her bed. We laughed and shared for hours before we noticed the time.

"Sean, I'm really enjoying myself and I hate to leave, but I really should be getting back. My ex has the children and I need to check on Benita as well.

"No, it's okay….I understand, I'm just thankful that God willing we'll be able to pick up where we left off, next weekend," Sean pulled my chair out for me to get up.

We walked hand in hand all the way back to his car laughing and talking.

Leon must have called my phone 111 times and Michael had called several times as well. But there was 1 number that popped up that I didn't realize. I made a mental note to check my voice mail as soon as I got home.

Over the next few weeks leading up to Memorial Day weekend, I was spending a lot of time with Sean. Leon and I were still seeing each other intimately at least once a week. I don't know why, but he still had a hold on me in some sort of a way. He didn't make me feel special anymore, but I still had some weird really undefined type of feelings for him. It seemed like he accepted the fact that I was unable to be at his beck and call any more. It was almost like I was a matter of convenience for him. Sort of like, well since I'm in the area let me call up Kiyah and get hit off! That's exactly what that *sheisty*, fake behind pimp is thinking.....Oh Lord what am I going to do?

*'Father, what am I doing lately? I know I'm making all kinds of bad choices right now but my mind is racing and I'm just searching and searching and yet I don't know what it is I'm looking for....JESUS,'*

Every now and then I needed to talk to the Lord, I wasn't sure he would hear me especially the way that I've been going lately. I don't know but one thing's for sure - as soon as I get back from Cancun, I'm going to completely break things off with Leon. Most of my time had been consumed by Sean lately anyway. Every weekend we went somewhere to do a little shopping and I was really starting to like him. Sandy was intensely jealous of all the time I was spending with Sean. She really didn't know that it was Sean I was spending time with, but she did sense that it was a man. Sandy knew that only a man could keep me from gossiping with her every night like clockwork.

It was Sunday leading up to Memorial Day weekend, three weeks since they had released Benita from the hospital. The doctors said that it was only a matter of time. Instead of going to my own church, Sean had invited me to go to church with him. Wow, this really took him up a notch. With Leon I couldn't visit his church 'cause our relationship was a secret. I was thinking that this thing with Sean may turn out to be just what I needed. It felt so liberating when Sean insisted on picking me up so that we could arrive together at his church. Just like a real couple. I felt valuable around Sean and clean for some reason.

Although I had just been with Leon sexually last night, it still seemed like we were drifting miles and miles apart. On the other hand, Sean was refreshing, warm, honest and certainly sincere - but there was *something* with Leon that was nagging at me. I didn't like the idea that for the last week he wasn't calling much. Even after sex, he didn't beg for me to stay the night with him any more. As a matter of fact, it seemed like he was rushing me out last night, like he had other plans. Maybe the bum was really trying to make things work with his wife and was going back home last night. But the clincher was that he didn't even offer to give me some pocket change like he normally did. Something was up with him and I didn't like it!

Part of me wanted to get Leon out of my life, but now that he's not chasing me anymore, I'm sort of jealous, but of what?...I just don't know. There's something going on with him and knowing Leon; this is the time that I should be the most careful.

# Chapter 10
*What the....!*

Sean was looking just like fine wine this morning for church with his cranberry colored suit with thin gray pin-stripes. His light gray shirt with the burgundy, gray and white patterned tie was so well matched up. I couldn't have done a better job myself. Of course, I was done. I didn't want to over do it though, especially since it was my first visit to his church. I figured it wouldn't be good for all of his admirers to hate me right off the bat. I wore a bone knitted suit with matching floppy wide-brimmed hat from Neiman Marcus. Only Calvin Klein Ultra Sheer off- white stockings would do to compliment the look of this outfit. Oh well let them hate me, 'cause I couldn't resist putting on my cream satin pumps with the heels totally made out of rhinestones that just so happened to bring out the extra large rhinestone buttons that rested on the jacket of my suit.

When Sean and I walked in the sanctuary, all eyes were on us. It felt really good. He was putting me on parade, unlike Leon who always wanted to sneak around because everything had to be hidden to protect his reputation. This was what I needed - a man that had nothing to hide.

As we made our way to our seats, the choir was up singing and WOW! It must have been at least 60 people up there. They sounded like a heavenly army. The church was huge like ours, but more like a theatre. It must seat at least 1,500 people comfortably. The choir was singing "The Spirit of the Lord is Here" and Oh! My God - it certainly was. The congregation was on their feet and the choir director, a well dressed man, was giving us a full fledged performance. Funny, I expected him to be a woman by what Sean had mentioned during one of our conversations. Ummn, maybe this was somebody new, quite naturally they wouldn't let the young lady Sean was referring to, continue to take on such a position in the church while sleeping around with some of the members. I made a mental note to ask Sean about this later.

Anyway *Mr. Honey*, I mean the choir director was just sashaying and dancing and jumping and putting so much emotion into his directing of the choir it was more, I mean *more* than entertaining. I don't know if anybody else in there could tell, but you would have to be blind not to see that *"That Thing"* was gay as a humming bird. But he was sharp though! The choir had on black and white Robes with the initials of the church's name going down the front left side in silver letters. But he (the choir director) had on a black suit. The pants were a little tight and the jacket was long with a sort of drawstring look around the waist. The long cuffs from the sleeves of his white 'Poet's Style' dress shirt hung over his hands as they extended far past the sleeves of his suit jacket as he was throwing them up and down dramatically while directing the choir. That's one thing that I do admire about *"The Fruity Kind"* they take it to the next level when it comes to performing, dressing and decorating.

I enjoyed watching him perform but I noticed Sean was bothered by his antics, 'cause more than once while he (the choir director) was performing, he(Sean) was huffing and puffing like he was just too annoyed.

Sean's minister gave a great sermon. It was easy to see where Sean got his training from. I stood up when they asked visitor's to stand. The pastor asked if anyone would like to have anything to say and of course I did. Mainly to enlighten every single female in the place that 'yes' Minister Sean was now taken and secondly to make sure they got a good look at my outfit.

"Praise the Lord everyone. My name is Ms. Kiyah Simmons and I bring you greetings from Christian Holiness Full Pentecostal Church where my pastor is Bishop, Dr., District Elder Simmons in Irvington, New Jersey. I am here visiting with Minister Sean Johnson. I really enjoyed your sermon today Pastor and I look forward to worshipping with you all again. God Bless You All!" I said in my most eloquent voice. When I mentioned Sean's name, his pastor's facial expression showed his approval. Sean was blushing all over himself and why wouldn't he? It's no secret that I made him look good.

After service, Sean took me up front to greet his pastor and first lady personally. While we were waiting to get to them, the choir director was steadily calling Sean.

"Sean, don't even try it," the director said snapping his neck at Sean with his hands on his hips.

"What are you talking about Devin?" Sean replied back.

"Come here and introduce your little friend," Devin said now laughing.

"She doesn't want to meet you. We're waiting to talk with pastor." Sean turned around to grab my hand and help me up to the pulpit where his pastor and first lady were seated. Quite a few people were ahead of us and I noticed that certain people the deacons wouldn't even allow past a certain point. Sean must have been in very good standing with the ministry 'cause they didn't even question him.

"DON"T GET CUTE SEAN," Devin said as he walked over closer towards us. "Since Minister Sean doesn't know how to mind his manners, my name is Devin *honey*, what's yours?"

"Kiyah," I answered.

"Kiyah….how cute," Devin said sounding very, very phony. I started to let him have it but I wouldn't dare show out in front of Sean's pastor. Besides I knew how gay men could be, so I just chalked it up to the defect.

"Look Devin, stop playing. For real don't play with my girl like that. All that stuff you do - it's funny and all but not right now....I'm serious, go head," Sean was annoyed, I could tell 'cause I had never heard him talk like this before. I knew gay guys could rub straight guys the wrong way and very easily, so I understood why Sean had gotten a little heated with Mr. Devin."

"Your *GIRL!* Oh really." Devin had a surprised smirk on his face.

"YOU HEARD ME," Sean responded now with a lot more

bass in his voice. "Go head about your business and leave MINE alone, You play too much, y'all don't know how to act when somebody brings a guest around."

"Why are you being so touchy? I was just kidding....I'm sorry Ms. Whatcha ma callit, Kee-yah, whatever ....I didn't mean anything by what I said.... Sean and I kid around a lot....but I guess he's just not in the mood for it today.... especially since he has *company*....and to tell you the truth I don't give a rat's behind what Minister Sean is the mood for (he said rolling his eyes in a way that only a gay man could roll his eyes) and then he turned to me and said..... "But I WILL be nice only 'cause you are company."

"Come on Kiyah we're next to talk to Pastor Brown," Sean said while pulling me around to him and away from Devin.

We met and talked with his Pastor and first lady. Sean introduced me as his *"Girlfriend"*....His pastor was pleased and mentioned how beautiful I was. Pastor Brown's wife didn't say much, but smiled pleasantly the whole time. Leon's wife should take lessons from her instead of frowning and growling at every attractive woman in the congregation that she fears is sleeping with her husband.

Well I guess that Sean and I had finally defined our relationship. *"Girlfriend,"* so I guess that makes him my *"Boyfriend"*. That sounds so grade school. Anyway, we went out to eat after church and I really enjoyed myself. During dinner Sandy called to let me know that my ex (Michael) came to our church today and was looking for me. Oooh that made me feel real, real good. Even though

Michael had been very nice and considerate with helping me with the kids lately, I still enjoyed him having to wonder where and what I was doing; just like I had to do when we were together. I really wanted to get all the dirt from Sandy, but I couldn't be rude to Sean. He was so sweet and besides he's now officially *my boyfriend.*

"Sandy, I'll call you back. Minister Sean and I are having dinner."

"MINISTER SEAN?....You church hopping skeezer....So that's who you've been spending all your time with lately. I guess you can't leave those darn ministers alone, that's pitiful. Girl, call me back as soon as you get home. We've got some catching up to do," Sandy shouted through the phone. Lord, I hope that Sean couldn't hear her loud mouth through the phone.

"Bye. I'll call you later."

Yes! It felt good to tell Sandy that I was out *in public* with my man. I knew this thing with Sean and I was right. I actually felt *saved* all day long.

"Kiyah, excuse me, but this is Pastor Brown calling me otherwise I wouldn't take the call," Sean stated while pulling his cell phone from his waist.

"Sure, go ahead."

After a few moments of conversation, Sean hung up and explained, "Sweetheart, Pastor just asked me to deliver next

Sunday's morning sermon. Kiyah! Do you know what this means? I knew that it was a blessing to have you in my life, but God is just confirming it. Everything has been going so well for me, especially in my ministry since I've met you. There's an associate pastor position up for grabs at our church and by Pastor asking me to speak next Sunday, it's a good indication that I'm the one he's considering for the job." Sean grabbed my hand enthusiastically.

"Great, honey." I replied, while thinking that a hug or kiss would have been more suitable for celebration. My God; leave it up to me to go from one minister that can't keep his hands to himself to another that doesn't know when and how to use his hands.

Queen had called several times during dinner, so I thought I should answer just in case something had happened with Benita.

"Hello," I answered.

"Yeah, that sorry behind ex husband of yours had the nerve to come to church this Sunday and finally sit through a whole sermon," Queen complained. "After service I brought the kids home with me. I wasn't about to let him take those kids to go running the streets. They needed to eat some home cookin' and you - you need to start spending more time with those kids. Kyasia's getting older and you better start keeping a closer eye on her. She's developing, got a little shape and she shouldn't be spending the night out. I don't care if it is her father. You don't know what's going on over there where he's staying. Lord, mommy is probably turning over in her grave. Anyway, Benita ate a little bit today and sat up for a little while. I don't know Kiyah, you're going to regret not sitting your hot tail down somewhere and trying to be a mother to those children. I got a feeling that you're still seeing that poor excuse for a preacher, Leon! I know you. You don't come around us, when you're doing wrong. If I find out - I mean it! - I'm going to be finished with you!"

Boy! She could go a mile a minute with her mouth. I'm thirty-three years old and I felt like I was being scolded by my mother. She's my sister and I respected her too much to interject.

Sean didn't mind. he was just so ecstatic that his pastor had asked him to speak next Sunday. I don't think it would have mattered to him whether I stayed on the phone or not. However, I didn't want to be rude, so I needed to reassure Queen and get off the phone quickly.
   "Queen, I went to church this morning with Minister Sean and now we're having brunch. So this really isn't a good time to discuss things. Hopefully, I've answered some of your accusations. If not, I will certainly put the others (accusations) to rest at a more appropriate time," I was being cute and I knew she could tell.

"Don't be *smart* Kiyah! Well....maybe I was wrong to accuse you of still seeing Leon. But, you went to church with this guy? Seems like this one is off to a good start, huh?....Oh! let me, let you go....don't worry about the kids. Call me when you're on your way to get them." Queen really wanted the scoop. I know it took all her dignity to allow me to get off the phone.

After we finished dinner, Sean asked if I wanted to catch a matinee with him, but I had already caught feelings from the things Queen said regarding my children. I was ready to go home, so I declined.

Sean walked me to my car and *finally* gave me a hug. I wondered was it just his spirituality that caused him to not hold me tight the way Leon did. His (Sean's) hugs felt like something I would give a platonic friend. Anyway, we said our good-byes and I was off.

I wasn't in my car 10 minutes before my cell phone rang and the screen read, *Leon's office*. Well let's make that I felt saved for almost a whole day. This call came right on time, 'cause Sean left me lacking in the intimacy department. For once I was glad to see that it was Leon calling me. My body missed him.
"Hello," I purred in my seductive tone.

"Don't try to sound sexy, WHORE! I know my husband is with you. I should have *whooped* your behind in New York. I hope you're proud that you have destroyed our family. You're a poor excuse for a mother, you desperate piece of trash! Tell my husband that as we speak I'm holding a meeting with the board of trustees, here at the church," Tonya, (Leon's wife) scowled into the phone.

"*Excuse me*, who's desperate? He's *your* husband and you're calling me - asking *me,* to give him messages for you. What's the matter Mrs. Booker? Are you mad 'cause I'm such a *good whore* that you have to come through me to

145

get a message to your husband?" I teased. I'm tired of her now and I felt that she had been overdue for a good *telling off!*

"Just give him the message *slut*! By the way I have good news for you Kiyah! You can have him now. Since you wanted him so bad, I hope you have a good job, 'cause Leon only likes the best. Somebody's got to be able to afford his lifestyle, 'cause I'm going to rake him so dry, when I get finished with him, there won't be enough money left to buy an ice cream cone," she laughed. I didn't think it was funny.

"Oh no girlfriend, I never said I wanted him. As long as y'all was together and his finances was in tact - he was alright with me. Trust me. I'm not applying for your position, 'cause I don't do dishes or iron shirts. I am a DIVA and will be treated accordingly."

There was a time that I prayed that Leon would leave his wife and marry me. More than once I dreamed of that fairytale wedding, house and picket fence. But now - I didn't know what I wanted. Leon definitely wasn't the man that I thought he was ten months ago. He still had a sexual hold on me and I sunk at the thought of him wanting anyone else besides me. But now all of a sudden I couldn't even picture a life with him anymore. I know I'm way past wrong right now 'cause *he is* her husband. But I'm tired of his wife calling me everything *but* my name. I couldn't even think, because she was still screaming in my ear.

"You've spent the night out with him for the last two weeks, but all of a sudden you don't want him. NOT without all the money huh?  I figured he would find out soon enough what a gold digging tramp you are," she snarled.

"Your mamma's a tramp!" I snapped

"I didn't call to argue with you. I don't talk to trash; I have it thrown out! Just tell Leon that he'd better get his cheating, lying behind over to this church asap." she slammed the phone down.

She just burst my bubble. 'Cause I have only seen Leon twice in the last two weeks. Instantly pain crept into my heart at the thought of Leon being with another woman. I didn't even get a chance to break up with him first. That *dirty bastard!*....was cheating on me *and* his wife!

## CHAPTER 11
### *All Hell Brakes Loose!*

I don't know why I felt so awful and couldn't function after finding out that Leon was seeing somebody else. I had planned on leaving him *anyway*, but him moving on *first* wasn't part of my plan. Sitting in front of Queen's house, I couldn't resist calling him.

It rang twice before his voicemail picked up. That sneaky little bum pushed ignore on his cell phone. I hope he realizes that I know that if a cell phone is turned off, it will go directly to voicemail, but when it rings first and then goes to voicemail - that means that the party you're calling is screening their calls and has chosen not to take it (your call). Just wait till I catch up with Leon Booker. I was now in a state of emotional frenzy. Kyasia must have noticed me sitting in front of Queen's house, because she came out to the car.

"Mom, what are you doing?," she asked through the car window.

"Nothing,…sweetie. Just making a few calls."

"Why don't you come inside and use Auntie's phone?"

"I'm fine honey. I already finished anyway." I got out the car and walked over to Kyasia.

"Mom, Daddy was looking for you at church this

morning. Why weren't you there?" Kyasia questioned with disappointment.

"I went to church with a friend Kyasia. I didn't know your dad was coming to our church today."

"You don't know anything, anymore mom. You don't care! Daddy has been doing good lately, but you've been too busy to notice!"

"Kyasia!, you betta watch who you're raising your voice at, before I have to get *on* you! I can see you're upset and I want you to express yourself to me, but you better make sure that you do it in a respectful way. I'm still your mother. Do you understand me, young lady?"

"Yes, I'm sorry, Ma….but Daddy has been trying hard. He's working and he's really trying to get our family together again, but you're never around to give him the chance," Kyasia said through tears.

I knew that Michael and I getting back together is something that both of my kids have wanted for a long time. They didn't understand the things that I had been through with their father. I never told them. I never wanted to talk bad about their father to them. I would do anything for my kids, but taking Michael back - I just couldn't see myself doing that. I wasn't even attracted to him anymore. It would make the kids so happy. Maybe I could try, I don't know.

I hugged Kyasia to console her and I thought of how life was before my marriage to Michael had crumbled. We were so happy. Towards the end, I wasn't happy - but they (my kids) were. And right now, I think that's the most important thing. Maybe it would be better if at least I could do something to make them (the kids) happy. Nothing seems to be working out for me anyway, except for Sean. Oh Lord! I totally forgot all about him for a minute. That's scary. How could I forget about him? He's after all - *my boyfriend.*

As much as I wanted to ease Kyasia's hurt, I couldn't take Michael back. I'm with Sean now.

"Mom, daddy's bringing our things over to the house tonight. Will you please talk to him? Pleassse?! I want us to be a family again. I don't like growing up without my father," my daughter pleaded while holding me tight.

"Okay, honey....stop crying. Everything is going to be fine. I promise!"

"You promise? Mom you promise to give Daddy another chance?" Her eyes were filled with hope.

"I can't promise that, sweetheart. But I promise you that everything will be fine. I know how you feel honey and I...."

"YOU DON'T KNOW! You grew up with your father in the same house with you. Whenever you needed him he was right there. How do you think I feel when my father isn't there on father and daughter day at my school? How do you think I feel when I have to page him and wait days for him to call back? I feel awful when Daddy doesn't come by and see us, 'cause he's mad at you for dating other guys. WHY can't you do this for us? I get good grades. I keep my room clean. I'm not perfect mom, but I try. I try so hard to be perfect for you so that you will love me like you used too, before you met *Leon*," she cried.

"*Oh Kyasia*, I love you more and more everyday. What are you saying sweetheart? Do you think that I love you less than I did before? That's not possible. You're my daughter; I couldn't love anything or anyone more than I love you and your brother." I didn't even realize that Kyasia knew about my relationship with Leon. She's almost thirteen, very mature and it was only a matter of time before she started taking notice of what's going on around her.

"Yes you do! You love Leon more than you love us. Mom when you thought I was sleep, I saw you sneak out in the middle of the night to go out with *him*. Everytime I heard your cell phone ring late at night, I knew you was going to leave us and go to him. I'm the one that had to rub Kaseem's back when he had nightmares and you weren't there. I know that you're gonna leave us one day *for good* to go and be with Leon. **I hate him**! He's the reason why you won't take Daddy back. That's why I called his wife and told her on him."

"YOU DID WHAT?!....How did you know? How did you get her number?"

"I got his church number out of your cell phone. Everybody knows that Leon's married mom. I hated when people talked about you at our church. Mom, Leon is the devil. I know he gives you nice things. But I could get a job when I turn fourteen…."

I had to stop her because she was breaking my heart.

"You don't have to get a job, honey. It's *my job* to take of you and your brother. I would *never* leave the two of you, for anyone, I'm sorry…." Reality dropped with the tears that were now running down my face and landing on my daughter's forehead as she looked up at me with her own eyes flooded with water. I'm not a good mother. I failed. How could I have done this to my children. I have put a lot of responsibility on this child. Always having her look after her brother while I was busy running the streets with Leon's no good a--.

"Kiyah! I didn't know you were here? I was wondering where Kyasia had drifted off too. What's wrong?" Queen yelled from her doorway.

"Nothing, I pulled up about 10 minutes ago. Everything is okay. We'll be right in."

"Okay, come on. The food is all done and I want us to sit down and eat together," Queen insisted.

"Alright," I yelled back. Then I turned Kyasia's face up to mine and asked, "Are you okay?"

"Yes,"

We went inside Queen's house where the majority of the

family was. We always met over here on Sunday's to eat. I didn't have to wonder long where Ever Ready was, because she called not long after I had arrived.

"Kiyah, Ever Ready wants you on the phone," Queen informed as she walked from the kitchen into the den where I was sitting with my kids and about a dozen of my other nieces and nephews watching BET.

"Hey, What's up?" I grabbed the receiver to speak to Ever Ready.

"Queen told me you went to church with that minister that spoke at noon day service a few months ago. What's up with that?"
Ever Ready inquired.

"We're dating, but I can't talk about that now. I'll see you when you get here. How long are you going to be?"

"That's the thing, I'm not coming. The Mass Choir was asked at the last minute to sing downtown Newark on Broad St. at Bishop Holmes church. It's his anniversary. I'm trying to round up as many members of the choir that I can. I know that it's going to be nothing but a competition. So I could use as much support as I could get." I knew where she was going with this. She was the President of our music department and was always committing to things without consulting with the rest of the choir.

"And….?" I questioned.

"And I need you to bring your voice down here and help us out. Service starts in about two hours."

"I can't, Ev. I just got here and Queen has already been fussing about me not spending enough time with the kids."

"I've already talked to Queen about it and she's willing to keep the kids. Don't mind her, she's always preaching to us about our kids. She forgets about when she was running the streets and mommy was watching her two. Anyway, come on Kye, this is for the church. You know Queen isn't going to have a problem with that," she persisted.

"Hold on, let me ask her....Queen! Ev wants me to meet her downtown to s....," I was in the midst of yelling when Queen interrupted by hollering back from the kitchen.

"Yeah, yeah. I know. She was just telling me about it. Go 'head, y'all get on my nerves. Just bring yourself right back here when it's over. Y'all don't think I *ever* get tired of babysitting," Queen fussed.

"Alright, Ev. She's fussing but she's seems to be okay with it. I've had a heck of an afternoon. So, I'm going to eat and relax for a few minutes. I'll be there on time," I explained.

As I was hanging up with Ever Ready, Kyasia was looking dead in my mouth.

"Mom, did you forget Daddy was coming over tonight? *Remember!"* Kyasia reminded me. After what just took place I couldn't disappoint her.

"What time? Did he give you a time sweetie?"

"He said around nine but knowing Daddy, it will probably be more like 9:30."

"Okay, no problem. It's 2 o'clock now. The service that Aunt Ev wants me to go to starts at four. So I should be good and finished by eight at the latest. Alright pumpkin?.... and we will be home long before nine, okay?" I tried to reassure my daughter.

With a bright smile, Kyasia gave me a big hug. "Okay, Mom. Go 'head and have a good time."

"Well, could I at least eat with you guys first before you throw me out?" I said teasingly.

Queen had put her foot in those mustard greens, pot roast, macaroni & cheese, potato salad, fried chicken, seasoned rice and corn bread. I was in la' la' land on Queen's den sofa by 3 o'clock sound asleep when my cell phone rang. It was Sandy.

"Hey Girrrlll, are you going to Bishop Holmes church? Your sister just called me."

"Yes, I'm going,"

"Good, 'cause I need a ride," Sandy explained.

"Where are you? I'm not driving way down into the Net.

I'm right here at Queen's house, only ten minutes away from downtown."

"Calm down. I'm in Irvington Center on Springfield Avenue at that new buffet place,"

"Okay, I'll pick you up in 20 minutes. Ev wants us to get there early enough for Tarasha and Neesha (our choir directors) to run through a couple of songs with us," I informed.

"Okay, I'll be outside. Thanks."

"Alright," I hung up the phone and dozed back off for a few more minutes of cat napping.

## CHAPTER 12
### *Fireworks*

I picked Sandy up and we arrived at Bishop Holmes church at least 30 minutes before service was due to start. Ever Ready did a good job rounding up members of the choir. It must have been at least forty of us there. Our musicians Junior and Jay Jay were on their way. We rehearsed in the parking lot of the church until Ev was satisfied.

The church was packed in no less than 45 minutes flat. They had us placed on the program to go up right before the preacher for the evening. Ever Ready was seated in the pulpit while the rest of us sat on the left side of the sanctuary towards the middle. She was on the program to respond to the welcome address. As I was scrolling down the program I got totally shocked. I nudged Sandy.

"Look, whose speaking this afternoon," I whispered pointing to the spot on the paper where Leon's name was printed next to God's Word.

"Get the hell out of here!....Oops! excuse me Lord. Get out of here, Leon's speaking Wow!"

"I didn't expect that, this should be interesting," I said feeling anxious.

"I know he's going to be shocked to see us after all of this time," Sandy continued. Little did she know that it hasn't been long *at all* since Leon had seen me.

After a few choirs had sung (including ours) and a couple of people gave a few words of exhortation - Leon came waltzing down the aisle with his entourage. Paul was right behind him with at least 5 other guys. This nigga really thought he was a star. I turned to look the other way because I just couldn't look him in his face as he was approaching my row.

"Kiyah! Look! He had the nerve to bring that girl he is messing with," Sandy whispered.

I turned around to see the young lady Sandy was referring to, walking behind the last guy in Leon's crew. When she(the girl) finally got up close. I couldn't believe it. It was that nasty huzzie from Jezebel's, Ms. Amy! What in the world was she doing here?.... *and* with Leon?

"That's the singer from New York. A lot of people thought she was from Newark 'cause she travels with Evangelist Bonner. Everyone's talking about her affair with Leon. The nerve of him to parade her up in here," Sandy said almost pinching the skin off of my arm.

"*She's* the singer I heard he was messing around with over 6 months ago?" I questioned.

"Yes, that's her and she thinks her sh--don't stink," Sandy paused and continued. "I heard she was crazy about him too."

I couldn't even respond. I was in shock. That's why she was so irritated when Leon and I met at Jezebel's. Who knows what excuse Leon had given her for our meeting. He could lie his way out of a double pad-locked iron box. So far I wasn't noticed. Paul was busy attending to Leon and Amy sat amongst the other five guys perched in the front row. That bi--- must have thought she was me.

Finally, Leon got up to speak,

**"Praise the Lord Everyone. Oh come on let's give God some praise up in this place! He's worthy, He's WORTHY. Come on Zion. Give Him some praise!** But before I go any further I'm going to call on a beautiful young woman of God who thought it not robbery to come here tonight and bless us with her angelic voice. So before we hear from the Lord tonight, Sister Amy Washington will deliver our sermonic solo. Come on y'all, make her feel welcome. Sister Amy," Leon said as he moved over from the pulpit to help Amy up to the podium. What a gentlemen. Humph! That phony fake a-- wanna be preacher is going to get a good piece of my mind tonight. Oooh! The nerve of him, advertising his affair up in the house of God. I've had enough.

Just as Leon was helping Amy up to the podium, he spotted me and had the nerve to wink his eye at me. That *bastard* is a trip! I had a phone call to make. I excused myself and went to the bathroom to make one very important call.

When I came back, Amy was up there singing, *"I won't complain."* I must admit she is a good singer, but her drama just wouldn't stop. She was one of those dramatic gospel singers. This chick really put on a performance – extending her arms, throwing back her head and clasping her belly when she held certain high notes. This heifer thought she was the 'prima of Gospel. As she belted out the last verse *"I've had some good days and I've had some bad days. BUT GOD, God has been good to me, Better than this ole' world could ever be. And I won't, I won't COMPLAIN!"* Most of the people in the sanctuary were on their feet, which was a good thing, 'cause she didn't even notice me as I was taking my seat. "Hallelujah! Come on and worship Him. Glory to God!….hallelujah!" Amy said as she passed the microphone back to Leon.

"I WON'T COMPLAIN. I CAN'T COMPLAIN. GOD HAS BEEN *GOOD* TO ME!" Leon said looking lustfully at Amy as she walked back to her seat. He just ain't no good. Sandy nudged me immediately. That's a shame that he would use God's platform to glorify his indiscretions.
"HE'S BEEN BETTER TO ME THAN I BEEN TO MYSELF. I DON'T KNOW ABOUT YOU, BUT I *CAN'T* COMPLAIN," Leon already had the church in an uproar. Even Ever Ready was up on her feet praising God.

By the time service was over and most of the people had cleared out of the sanctuary, I made my way up front to have a word with Mr. Magic (Leon). At first I was just going to speak politely but something just rose up inside of me. Paul got nervous as he noticed me approaching Leon, but he dared not try and stop me,
"Leon, I didn't expect to see you here….and especially *not* with Amy," I inquired.

"Kiyah, this is about ministry. What are you suggesting? Look, how about discussing this later at your house?" Leon was trying to get rid of me as he saw Amy approaching. At first she was meeting and greeting with some other church folk. But once, she noticed me talking with Leon, she made a bee-line right over to us.

"No, Leon! You're not coming over my house and we don't need to discuss anything *anymore*," I said looking at him with disgust. I tried real hard to keep my tone low.

"What's going on!" Amy questioned, while placing her body right between Leon and I, with her back facing me *again*. This chick was asking for a beatdown.

"Nothing. Kiyah just needs to talk to me about something," Leon explained.

"I don't care *what* she wants to talk to you about. I let that little *so-called* important counseling session at Jezebel's pass, but I warned you then - no more. You're here with me and I'll be damned if she's gonna come up in here disrespecting me like that," The New York Bit-- had finally came out in Amy.

"Look, I'm a man of God. I have to counsel people everyday. I won't tolerate you acting like this - disrespecting and being rude to people while I'm ministering to them," Leon said trying to be slick.

"Pastor this doesn't look good. People are starting to stare and I think we should get out of here while they're still guessing," Paul suggested while grabbing Leon's arm to escort him out the sanctuary, but Amy's bold a-- couldn't let it go.

"What do you mean disrespecting her, Leon? I don't have to respect her. She's not your wife!" Amy demanded.

"BUT I AM!" Tonya (Leon's wife) had surprisingly walked up on Amy. What took her so long? I had called her over an hour ago. "I'm his wife, slut! Are you going to respect me? So you're the one that has been sleeping with my husband. I guess he has you to thank for being homeless tonight," Tonya said with her hands on her hips.

I stepped back 'cause this was going to be a bull dog fight. Amy was brazen, Tonya was exasperated and I didn't give a damn.

"Come on Tonya, cut this out. Let's talk about this at home. I'm not sleeping with anybody, *honey*. Stop this. Let me take you home? God just used me to bless His people like never before in this place and this is just like the devil. He's mad. That's why he uses circumstances to cause your mind to think such horrible thoughts. I love you, Tonya. Why do you keep accusing me of such things?"

"Leon!....*what* are you talking about. You keep promising me that you're going to leave your wife. Well now's as good time as any. Tell her, tell her Leon....I'm tired of sneaking around with you. We've been seeing each other for over a year now. Why don't you just tell her?" Amy demanded.

"I don't know what you're talking about? Blasphemy! I've told you no such thing. You must be sick....Look Tonya, she accompanied me to a few services to sing but that's it. Look...." Leon tried to plead with Tonya but she wasn't buying it.

"No more Leon! No more of your lies. It's over. I have a good mind to kick you where the sun won't shine. But today I realize that you're not worth it. You were never worth it! I don't know what kind of beast you are? God is going to reckon with you one day soon. For the last 18 years you have put me through so much humiliation and emotional distress. All of your lies....so many times I've caught you with other women....but I wanted to believe your excuses, because that's the only thing that ever made sense to me. You had no reason on this earth to humiliate and make mockery of our marriage, the way you have done. I stuck by you and worked two jobs while you went to seminary school. Then you repay me by sleeping with practically every decent looking woman that darkened our church door. Time and time again I had to pretend like I didn't realize what was going on right underneath my nose. Well, I can't pretend anymore. I'm exhausted from trying to hold my head up while people are talking and snickering behind my back. You have sunken to an all time low, when you utilize the house of God to carry on and glorify your affairs." Leon tried to interrupt Tonya as she was talking, but before he could get one word out she stopped him.

"Shut up Leon! Your gift of gab can't bail you out of this one. I've already met with the trustee board and made them aware that I am going to be filing for divorce. Your whores can finally have you, because I am *done*," Tonya walked away and made her way past two of Leon's boys to get out of the sanctuary. She looked at me with tears strolling down her face as she passed. It wasn't the same look of hate or contempt that I had experienced in New York, but in some sort of strange way – a look of gratitude.

Paul did a good job clearing all of the people out of the building in an effort to try and hide what was going on.

"Look at what you've done! If you've caused me....to loose my church, my ministry. I'll....Let's go Paul, get me out of here," Leon said angrily.

"You're not going anywhere! What you're gonna do?  Just leave me here like this, Leon?....you sorry bastard!" Amy screamed.

"I'm going home to my wife! Here's fifty dollars catch a cab or train or something," Leon smirked as he walked away with his back turned.

For the first time, I could tell that Leon was scared to death. I guess out of all the times his wife had caught him before, he could tell this time she was really through. My mother always told me that if a man can cause you to get upset and fight, he knows that he has you. But when you show him that you care more about yourself than him, that's when he'll realize that he's got to stay on his toes with you.

"You low-down dirty piece of sh--," Amy grabbed something out of her purse and lunged at Leon.

Paul tried to stop her by jumping in front of Leon as he turned around. All I saw was blood. Amy had stabbed Paul with a knife.

Ever Ready and Sandy burst into the sanctuary along with Bishop Holmes once they heard me screaming. Ever Ready came in swinging. She busted Leon all upside his head.

I was finally able to restrain Ev, before she permanently damaged Leon.

"Kiyah, what's wrong? What in the world is going on in here? I left you in here and went outside when this guy (Paul) laying here said that you guys had some business to discuss. I didn't feel right about it all along."

Next, I bent down to help Paul. "I think he's hurt."

"Don't move him!" Sandy screamed.

"I've got to go. Tee, grab my things," Leon ordered.

"What about Paul?" Leon's boy, Tee asked.

"What do you mean? *What about Paul?* I can't be involved in something like this. My reputation and career is at stake. *Man!* I've got to get out of here," Leon persisted holding his head. Ev had given him a few lumps.

"But what about Amy, Pastor? She doesn't look too good," Tee asked.

"I hope they arrest the crazy bit--!" Leon said as he motioned for Tee to hurry up and get him out of dodge.

Amy was crying, cussing and struggling like a beast, trying to break free from the church deacons, who were keeping her from leaving.

It was around 7 p.m. when the cops and paramedics came. They arrested Amy. Even though she was loud and ghetto as hell, I actually felt sorry for her. The paramedics determined right away that Paul's cut wasn't life threatening, but they took him to the hospital anyway to examine him.

✛   ✛   ✛   ✛   ✛

I dropped Sandy off, made it up to Queen's to get the kids, gave Queen the full scoop on what took place down at Bishop Holmes church and was still home by 9 o'clock.

Michael was there by quarter after. He came in and sat down and pleaded his case right away.

"It's no secret that I want to try and get my family back," Michael said.

"What's different this time?" I questioned.

"The difference is I have Christ in my life now....for real Kiyah. God has showed me how to be a better husband, a better father and a better friend," Michael seemed so sincere. This is one I hadn't heard before.

"We've been apart for quite some time Michael and I've changed. I can't even consider being with a man that is not willing to work and bring something to the table. It's hard enough for me trying to maintain and take care of these kids by myself."

"I plan on working and supporting both you and the kids. I already have a job working down at the docks in port Newark. I'm making over $15 an hour."

"That's good."

"The only problem is, I've been staying at my mom's; sleeping on the couch and it's hard getting any sleep while my nieces and nephews are up watching television. If I could just stay back here for a little while, I could pay half the bills. Which would make life a little bit easier for you and it would give us a chance to see if there's any possibility of working things out," Michael said looking down at the floor.

"I don't think so Michael. It's just too soon."

"Come on Kiyah, I miss you. Don't you miss me?" Michael moved close to me and began caressing my shoulders.

I know that I had a sexual demon, because I wasn't attracted to Michael and didn't want to be intimate with him - but I longed to be touched in a way that *only* a man could touch a woman. Michael's tender touching made me get wet instantly. I wanted him to take me upstairs and sex my brains out and then he could bounce. I knew that would be the wrong move with him. He would instantly think that was his ticket to move back in.

"Michael, I haven't been with you in over a year. It's not like that no more," I said pulling away.

"Is it someone else?"

"No, not right now," I lied.

"So what's the problem? We're still married and have our kids to raise….we should at least try for them."

I knew he was right. Michael and I getting back together would delight our children, but my sisters would be finished with me, especially Queen. She couldn't stand Michael, but Kyasia's been through a lot lately. Maybe I could try and just not tell my family right away. Besides, Kyasia's birthday is next week and this would brighten her spirits.

"Okay, Michael. You can stay here temporarily. Just to see how things go. And I'm not saying that we're getting back together," I warned.

"Thanks, Kiyah! You won't regret it. My life has been hell without you and the kids. I'm going to make you see that I have changed for the better," Michael said hugging me real tight. *'Now that's a man's hug,'* I thought as I was broke free from his embrace.

"Don't get carried away. This is just on a trial basis. You will reside on the couch after the children are sound asleep," I instructed. "You will not question my goings and comings.

I don't want you answering my phone, *house or cell*. When you get paid, I get paid! I mean it Michael! The first time you don't comply with these rules, I will have to ask you to leave: voluntarily or involuntarily," I said pointing to the phone. I had to remind Michael that I would call the cops on him in a heartbeat. He already has a bench warrant out for him for child support. Trust me, he didn't want no trouble.

"Alright….damn, Kiyah, you've gotten hard over the past year. I don't want us to have to go through nothing. I'm trying to make things right. So can I go tell the kids that their daddy is staying?," Michael said with excitement.

"Yes."

"Great!" he said as he picked me up in the air and twirled me around. He placed me back down on the carpet and raced upstairs to inform Kyasia and Kaseem. The kids were ecstatic, especially Kyasia. It scared me to death: the thought of Michael staying here, but the joy written all over Kyasia's face made it more than worth it.

✤    ✤    ✤    ✤    ✤

The smell of beef sausages sizzling in the skillet woke me up the next morning. As I unlocked my bedroom door to go downstairs, I remembered that Michael was here. Lord! I was hoping that it was all a dream.

Michael had the kids up and dressed. They were all sitting down eating. My plate was covered with another plate on the counter.

"Your sausages are done. You ready to eat?" Michael asked.

Who was he? This *wasn't* the Michael that I had been married to for fifteen years.

"Uh, yes," I stumbled in disbelief.

"Okay, sit down. Here's your sausage. I hope the grits aren't too thick?" Michael said as he poured my orange juice.

"They're perfect Daddy!" Kyasia gleamed.

"Thanks, Baby girl....You guys finish up so that I can drop you both off to school on my way to work. I don't want to be late." Michael winked at me.

"Huh, what time is it?" I asked.

"It's seven-thirty. I thought I would let you sleep late. Everything is on point. So you can take your time and relax for a change. You have plenty of time. You don't have to be to work until nine....right?" Michael asked while he was helping the kids clear their plates and get out the door.

"Well, yes...." I said confused.

After they left, I was almost scared to eat. He was being so nice. I thought maybe he had drugged me or something. Maybe Michael had really changed.

# Chapter 13
## *Same Dogs, New Tricks*

I arrived at work more confused than ever. Sandy greeted me with gossip.

"Hey Kiyah, I forgot to tell you last night with everything that was going on. But Miles brought his baby mamma to church yesterday," Sandy said while walking with me towards my desk.

"Get out of here! Miles doesn't even like church. So what made him come and *bring her* to our church?"

"I don't know, but they were all hugged up. I tell you one thing….they looked like the perfect little family. Yeah, they had little Miles with them."

"Well good for them," I said sarcastically.

"Alright, let me get back to work, before your sister comes in," Sandy said as she made a bee-line back to her desk which was up front. She seemed pleased with telling me about Miles coming to church with another female. What's this heifer up to?

Queen was a stickler when it came to the staff at the church being efficient. It was hard sometimes working for my sister. But most of the time it has its benefits.

Wow! Sandy's little comment caught me off guard. Since

Michael had come back on the scene, I barely talked to Miles.

"Kiyah," Sandy buzzed in on my phone.

"Yes,"

"It's Minister Sean on the blinking line."

"Thanks....Hello."

"Praise the Lord, beautiful," Sean sung into the phone. Boy was he happy.

"Praise the Lord. Boy! You're in a good mood this morning."

"Why shouldn't I be? God is good! I've called you early this morning to share some wonderful news with you. Late last night I got a call from my pastor. He told me that his Bishop called him and informed him that he's going to be asking one of his pastors in Teaneck to step down because of some big ruckus that broke out down at Bishop Johnson's church last night. Anyway, Pastor Brown said that it was a big commotion with this guy's wife, mistress and personal assistant. Somebody got hurt. It was just a mess. But the bottom line is, Bishop told Pastor that he would need someone to step in and oversee that ministry on his (Pastor Brown's) recommendation. And Pastor just told me that he is going to recommend me," Sean chided.

"Wonderful....Oooh, that's great," I said unenthused. This

is a remarkable coincidence.

"We've got to celebrate!....how about lunch at House of Plenty, in Union?"

"I can't, but why don't I drop by after work and we can celebrate then?" I tried to sound excited. First of all, I didn't feel good ever since Sandy had shared Miles *new situation* with me. Secondly, I needed some bad, this gave me a perfect excuse to get Sean alone and see if there's a iron-pumping behind this man. Look at me the man hasn't been installed yet and already I'm making plans to seduce him. It's a demon. A demon, *I tell you*!

"No problem sweetheart. I'll be home all day. Just give me a call before you come."

"Okay, I'll see you then," I said hanging up the phone.

The day had breezed by. And for the first time in over a year I didn't have to leave work, run get the kids and travel all the way back down to the church again. Earlier, Michael called and informed me that he would pick the kids up. Hmmn.....funny, how that negro could never find the time to help me out with our kids *before*. I guess since he knows first hand where the *kitty* is at night, he's willing to help the *kitty* out in the morning. Michael is a trip. He could be a good father as long as he's with me. You wouldn't have known he was related to my kids after we separated. *That bastard!* It just makes me mad every time I think about it.

But hey, I'm not going to complain. His long awaited help came right on time today, 'cause I was going to utilize this little time frame to go and pay Sean a visit. I was more than ready to consummate this relationship.

I was already in front of Sean's house when I realized that I forget to call him beforehand. Heck, he is *my boyfriend.* Why....should *I* have to be announced when coming to his house? I might as well see if the rat got some cheese stashed on the side. These slick men nowadays are always trying to keep their game under wraps. If Sean did have a little girlfriend on the side and was trying to be slick by making sure I call first. *Psych!* The jokes on him....because I'm already 10 feet from his door. When will these guys understand that I am the Diva that is *not* to be messed with. If he don't know, he better ask Leon. 'Cause I played his (Leon) three-timing, country a-- the hell out last night.'

But I seriously didn't think Sean was that type. But after all that I have been through, I couldn't help but think the worst. After my experiences with Michael, I find myself automatically suspecting every guy to be a cheat.

I was fixing my clothes as I approached Sean's apartment door. I could already hear soft music playing from inside his apartment. Wonder who he was entertaining? Luther was belting out a "A House Is Not A Home," when I knocked on the door. Sean turned the music down and I heard laughter. Now I was sure he had one of those little tramps from his church in there. Oooh! I'm going to bust his little *happy a-- *across his forehead. If it wasn't for shame, I would have peeked through the peephole.

"Who is it?" Sean asked while looking through his peephole.

"It's me, Kiyah. I'm sorry but my battery was dead on my cell, so I couldn't call before coming. I hope you don't mind?" I played it *cool*.

"Oh! NO, not at all….Just give me a minute to tidy up, Okay. Just *one* minute," Sean pleaded.

"Sure, no problem; but not ONE SECOND more."

I wonder how Sean is going to get out of this one. 'Cause I know he has a girl in there. *Darn,* were all these new ministers anointed with a cheating demon? *The prophecy of Lust*; I swear….I'm going to have to kill me a preacher, in a minute.

Sean is lucky, that I wasn't in too deep with him. 'Cause I would bust this darn door down, especially if he had already tapped this - but since we haven't gotten there yet, I wasn't even extremely hurt - just disappointed as hell. I almost expected this with him. He's young, good looking, a good preacher and *not* married. If Benita wasn't so sick, I'm sure she would have already gotten the scoop on this one and warned me well in advance.

The rattling of the door interrupted my thoughts.

"Come on in! Uh, you can have a seat," Sean said nervously.

"Thanks....It sounded like you had comp....," I stumbled in disbelief when I saw Devin, the choir director from Sean's church, standing on the other side of the living room with a deceiving smirk on his face. Now *this* I didn't expect.

"Hello *honey*, you look....well uh, anyway hi!" Devin whined while sashaying over to the couch. He was a horrible visual of Naomi Campbell – he nearly twirled his entire body before he poked out his butt and sat with his legs crossed, feet sharply pointed down and tilted his head with his nose stuck in the air.

I paid his gay a-- dust, since he wanted to give me *the business*. I ignored his fruit loop toting behind.

"Sean what is Devin doing over here?" I questioned.

"No! Ms. Thing! The question *IS*....what are *YOU* doing over here?" Devin said snapping his fingers in my face.

"You better get your hormonal infected fingers out of my face!" I stood up and over Devin, letting him know that I am not the one.

"Who are you calling infected? If I'm infected, then so is your little boyfriend over there!" Devin blasted.

Ooops! Somebody should have caught my face. 'Cause it had dropped like dead weight.

"Sean what in the *world* is he talking about?" I asked

walking over to Sean, who was sweating bullets by now.

"Devin please!....Look Kiyah, Devin came over here to run some....," Sean tried to explain while rubbing his head.

"Sean, why don't you grow some balls for a change? And don't Devin *please,* me!" Devin yelled back. "Fu-- that! Tell the little Tyra Banks *trying to* be! Besides, if she got any brains up underneath that weave, I know she can tell what's going on here. So you might as well tell her.

*Oh my God!* Sean and Devin sitting in a tree....*Ilk,* that's nasty. I'm not even mad that he's gay. One of my dearest friends is gay and I love him to death. I can't condemn him for that, for God loves the sinner, but hates the sin. But I *am* mad *as hell* that Sean lied to me. Got me all ready to test the waters and he's not even swimming in the same ocean.

"You....and Devin?...Sean tell me it's not true," I pleaded. He didn't answer, just hung his head down. "So that's why you loved to go shopping with me? 'Cause you're a freaking girl!" I screamed while pushing Sean.

"Okay honey, I know your little feelings are hurt and *oh my,* that's a shame. But don't go putting your claws on my man!" Devin grabbed me away from Sean.

"Devin you better keep your hands off of me!....before I slap you *into being a man!*" I snatched away.

Everything from that point on was a blur, because Devin and I started tussling. Sean got in between us and demanded that

Devin leave. I don't know why. He had a better chance with him. I don't want nobody that even *looks* at another man. Devin was furious at first and refused to leave. He gave in and left after Sean explained that he just wanted to talk to me. Sean told Devin that he at least owed me that much. Sean was silent for what seemed like an eternity. Then he finally walked over to the chair, facing the couch that I was sitting on, and flopped down in it.

"Kiyah....I don't really know what to say, But I...." Sean barely said.

"How about the truth?....plain and simple.    Why don't you start there?"

"Okay, I am bi....bisexual. But that doesn't mean that I'm a girl or not saved....Kiyah, I love the Lord! I live, breathe and eat the ministry. I constantly study the bible so that I can be better equipped to be a blessing to God's people." he paused and then continued. "I never meant to hurt you.... look, what Devin and I are doing....it's just not acceptable in the church, in public....it's just not acceptable."

"Alright, I can understand that. But why, did you have to involve me in this mess? If you have something with Devin, why bother pursuing me?....Damn, what's wrong with me? I must be a magnet for hurt, pain, and disappointment," I answered shaking my head.

"There's nothing wrong with you and I don't want you to think that way. You're beautiful, witty and a classy young woman. It's me. I try so hard to resist the feelings I have for

Devin. I've always had a problem, even admitting to myself that I am attracted to men. I hate that about myself. If I could change that *one* thing about myself, believe me *I* would. Ever since, I could remember, I was attracted to men. When I was 9 years old, my 16 year old male cousin, molested me. He forced me to perform oral sex on him and then went on to have sex with me. Ever since then I possessed this desire to be with men. I don't know....my life is over," Sean began to weep with his face in his hands.

"I know this is hard for you.... I'm not here to judge you. And I'm certainly not going to put your business on blast," I reassured.

"Thanks, I appreciate that."

We talked for a little while longer, and for some reason I knew we would always be friends. Sean was the type of guy that was so endearing; you just had to love him. He explained to me how the demon of homosexuality was the one thing that he could not conquer.

Finally I left Sean's house, still wanting to get hit off now more than ever. I needed to feel wanted and needed again. If I didn't get me some soon, I was going to explode.

When I reached home, Michael was going over homework with Kaseem. I don't know what in the world happened to my kids daddy?....because this had to be a clone.

"Hey, Lady....we've been waiting on you," Michael said approaching me.

He better back the hell up, because he's not my man.

"I don't remember asking you to wait on me....and for what?" I questioned. I don't want him to even think for one minute that he was gonna be clocking me. Besides, I probably would have arrived later than this, if Sean hadn't been frosted on one side.

"Naw, I'm not trying to put you on a curfew or nothing. I have dinner reservations for us at seven and it's a quarter too, now," Michael informed.

"First of all, you can't put me on a curfew.... so let's just get that straight, because this is my house and I have been footing the bills *alone* for the past year and a half. I can turn that key whenever I feel like, since I'm the only one that *feels like* paying the mortgage. Okay. And Michael let me just put you on the right path now, because I can see you're already falling off track. Do not take it upon yourself to make plans for me. Understand....as a matter of fact you know what? This is not going to work." I was already upset because my one chance at getting a little action tonight just so happened to be an undercover ballerina. I certainly wasn't in the mood for Michael to start acting like I had to answer to him.

"Okay, okay....calm down, it wasn't like that. What did I do? You act like I committed a crime. I thought I was being thoughtful by taking you out for dinner so that you wouldn't have to cook, especially after a long and hard day at work. I called myself being considerate. But you wanna come at me sideways and all I was trying to do was do something nice for you."

I felt really bad. I was really mad at myself, but I was taking it out on him. I looked around and noticed that the house was immaculately clean. I gagged; because not in all the fifteen years I was married to Michael did he lift one finger to clean. He was starting to make a believer out of me. Then an uncircumcised thought entered my head, *Michael is starting to look good to me.* Even though, he's a lying, cheating, sneaky, manipulating, conniving, non-working, morning breath in the evening time having jerk! He is a 100% man. I mean a real man….that I am certain of and as long as he doesn't try to kiss me in the mouth - the sex is guaranteed to be off the chains.

"Alright…. I did have a hard day, so maybe I'm just a tad bit agitated….Give me a minute to freshen up and I'll be right down," I said heading upstairs. When I put the key in the knob of my bedroom door, I was alarmed that it was already opened. I could have sworn I locked it before leaving out this morning. Maybe, I was mistaken. I quickly freshened up and changed.

We had a great time at dinner. I even considered giving Michael some tonight, but I was emotionally drained from all of the day's activities. So when we got back to the house, I hopped into a hot shower and went straight to bed. It was going to take more than a steak and clean house to travel up this road again.

Tuesday morning I arrived at work early and refreshed.

Since Michael was now feeding and taking the kids to school in the morning, I didn't know what to do with myself.

All day long I kept thinking about the things that had been happening in my life. Wow, I really thought I was better than this. First Michael and all of his cheating; how could I allow that man to cheat and spend all of my money at the same time? I wanted to reach back in time and slap my darn self. Well I guess he (Michael) knows now, that he's going to have to bring something to the table if wants to wiggle his way back in.

Then Leon - he takes the cake. He's nothing more than an anointed a-- hole. Just the thought of him made me want to cuss. Oooh, I couldn't stomach him. Leon is the kind of nigga that will cause you to commit a crime.
How couldn't I see, that he didn't care about anybody but himself? I foolishly expected this man to give me the respect I wanted; when he didn't even give his wife the respect she deserved.

Last but not least, there was Sean....what was I thinking about? I should have spotted the limp in his wrist from a mile away. The white car, all of the shopping excursions and he never tried to get any butt. Hell, I don't think he even glanced that way.

Darn, I missed Miles like crazy. I hadn't called him in practically a week. Now he's toting his baby mamma around. I done messed around and lost a hero, running after these no no's....I'm just sick.

By lunch time I was itching to call Miles. He had been on my mind all day. I felt extremely jealous at the thought of him with another woman. I didn't care if she was his baby momma.

Finally, by the time I punched back in from lunch, I had to call him.

"Hello," Miles laid back voice answered after only two rings.

"Hey, Dimples....what's up? I heard you paid us a visit on Sunday morning," I teased.

"Yeah, I thought I was going to see you there. What's up with you?"

Before I could answer Miles, Sandy beeped in on my intercom.

"Kiyah, I hate to interrupt you, but your sister's on line two and I....Well, I think you should take the call," Sandy said in a low almost nervous tone.

"Hold on Miles,.......Hello," I said after picking up line two.

"Kiyah! Get to Wali's house right away!"
Queen screamed into the phone.

"WHY? WHAT'S THE MATTER? It's Benita isn't it?," I yelled.

"Yes, I picked up Daddy and we're already on our way over there."

As Queen was hanging up my cell phone rang it was that darn 917 number. *'Why does this number always show up when I'm going through something?'* I figured I might as well answer it while Miles is still on hold.

"Hello,"

"Hello....is this Kiyah?" a compelling voice inquired.

"Yes, this is she."

"Oh, Wow! I finally caught up with you. I was starting to think you gave me the wrong number. I don't know if you remember me. My name is Shyne."

"Shyne?" (I knew exactly who he was, but I couldn't let him know that.)

"Yes, you met me in New York and....you gave me your number verbally and...."

"Yeah, okay. I know who you are now." I played it cool.

"So what's up, shorty?"

Beep! The office phone reminded me that I still had a call on hold. Ten minutes ago, I had struck out, but now I got two. So what's a girl to do?

"Shyne, I'm sorry but I'm right in the middle of a family situation. So can I call you back at this number?"

"No doubt….but look, I planned on being over in Jersey on Thursday and I was wondering if we could hook up?"

"That sounds good. You can meet me at my church, Christian Holiness Full Pentecostal at 1971 Clean Street in Irvington. I hate to rush you off the phone, but things are crazy right now."

"Don't worry about it gorgeous. I'll see you on Thursday, aiight?" Shyne hung up.

"Hello, Miles I'm sorry for having you on hold so long. It's just that….."

Beep! "Kiyah, girl I am so sorry to keep busting in on your calls, especially since you're talking to Miles." *'How in the hell did she know that?'* "It's Ever Ready and she doesn't sound good," Sandy interrupted.

"Okay Sandy, you can hang up now. I'll get it….Miles I'm sorry can you hold just one more second?" I apologized.

"Handle your business. I'm good."

"Thanks….Hold on….Ev, what's up?"

"Kiyah, they don't think Benita's going to make it. You better hurry!" Ever Ready was panicking.

"Oh God! I'm on my way right now." I clicked immediately over to Miles.

"Miles, I've got to go. It's Benita she's....well they think that she's not going to make it. Oh God, Miles! What am I going to do? I don't think I'm ready to deal with this," I started to cry.

"Are you okay?" Miles questioned.

"I don't know. I just got to go! Where are my darn car keys?" I was panicking.

"Slow down, Kye. I know you're upset but you've got to keep your focus." Miles was calm.

"Miles! How can I keep my focus when everything in my life is going wrong? And since that isn't enough, to top things off Benita is dying as we speak! I'm just...." I said now weeping.

"Kiyah I'm sorry....Look, relax and I'll be right there."

"For what?....I've got to go Miles," I said wimpering.

"Hold tight. You're in no condition to be driving. It will only take me five minutes to get to you." Miles hung up.

By the time I located my car keys, Miles was walking in looking like morning fresh dew. Instantly, his presence eased my sorrow.

As he walked pass Sandy and spoke. I could tell by the way her eyes followed him past her desk, that she was captivated by him.

"Well if it isn't *Super Thug*, rushing to his girl's rescue," Sandy couldn't resist teasing Miles. I was already making my way up to the front of the office.

"You know how I do," Miles said coolly.

"I found my keys. So you didn't have to rush over here...." Before, I could finish Miles interjected.

"Yo', I'm driving you and that's it. Let's go!" Miles demanded. He was so cool and it turned me on. I couldn't think about that now, nor did I have time to argue with Miles so I reluctantly went with the program.

"Okay, Thanks....What would I do with out you?" I said hugging Miles. This hug was different from all the other time. It was thrilling. But I could tell that he was giving me more than a hug. I don't know why, but it almost felt like a farewell. It scared me so bad, I quickly broke away.

"Well, if it isn't Clare and Cliff Huxtable. Could you'll please take the show on the road. I've got work to do and Kiyah....your family is waiting on you," Sandy chastised.

"I know....Come on Miles, where's your car parked?"

"Right out front....Sandy, I'm out." Miles said while

leaving.

When we arrived at Wali's house we noticed the family cars parked outside. Miles let me off in front and drove further down the street to find a parking space. The front door was open and from the walkway I could hear a murmur of prayer. As I approached the open doorway, I felt a solemn spirit surrounding the house. It was as if a dark cloud had overshadowed this place. I sensed death lurking around and waiting to make his move. I felt like I knew I was about to *robbed* but couldn't do anything about it.

Without waiting for Miles, I walked in. My family was standing around Benita's hospital bed praying. Benita's hospice nurse Rhonda, was talking to Wali on the side and letting him know that soon she would be suffocating on her own saliva and then it would be all over. In the meantime, she told him that he could keep giving her doses of morphine to relieve her pain. She explained to Wali that it didn't matter whether or not they over medicated her, because they just wanted her to be comfortable until she made her transition.

As Daddy overheard the conversation between Wali and the nurse, he lifted his head from praying and turned to face them.

"Young lady, I know you're in the medical profession and you are trained to make certain diagnosis, but I serve a God that specializes in making doctors out of liars. He does that every now and then to remind the doctors that He is God all by Himself. See young lady, my God don't practice medicine. He created medicine. He performs miracles. He heals the sick. He can raise the dead. His name is Jesus…. Hah Glory!….Wali you keep the faith. She's not going to leave here until God says so…."

"Mr. Simmons, I didn't mean…." Rhonda tried to explain before Daddy cut her off.

"That's okay young lady….I don't expect you to understand the type of faith I have. The only way you could, is if you knew my Jesus."

I grabbed Daddy when I noticed Benita trying to talk. She was struggling to sit up, but couldn't. It was amazing that she was still conscious. Her body was skeleton - thin, her light skin tone was now gray. She reached her hand up slowly to touch Daddy. With her eyes were closed, she just felt her fingers around the rail of her bed until her hand met with Daddy's hand. Benita's parents died when she was young, so she considered our parents to be hers. As she grabbed Daddy's hand, you could see the grimacing in her face. It was going to take all of her strength to speak. But you know Benita - she was going to give death a run for his money. The excruciating pain was evident as she kept moaning.

"uhn….uhn….dad….i'm….scared…. wanna….go…to…church," Benita was groaning with her eyes still closed and flickering.

"Daughter, we can have church right here. We don't need no building….The bible says that if two or three are gathered in His name, that He will be in the midst."

189

"No....dad....please....uhn....need.... make....it....to.... da....church....jus....one....more....time," Benita said now with her eyes half open and tears streaming down.

"Child, you're in no condition to be traveling. Don't worry, God is everywhere and He's here right now. He'll never leave or forsake you....you just hold on, God willing, we'll do what we can....Wali?....Queen?....Somebody! One of ya'll give her another dose of that medicine. Can't you see she's in pain?" Daddy scolded. He was hurting and this was his way of showing it.

"No....more....medi..cine, my last request....Wa...Wali..... I've got to make it....to the house of....the Lord," Benita pleaded biting her lip; forcing her body to relinquish some strength.

"I promise that I'll get you there. If you hold on until tomorrow, I will get you to the chur...." Wali tried to complete his thought. But the lump in his throat caused him to choke up. His pain was evident.

Benita immediately closed her eyes and rested. She was breathing extremely heavy. From what the nurse had explained to Wali earlier, I knew that the end was near.

I was distraught. Benita didn't even look the same. You could feel her anguish and desperation. I really couldn't believe that this was happening. Everyone was quiet. Miles came over to comfort me.

Wali walked over to Rhonda, who was reading Benita's stats, and pulled her to the side. "Is there anyway we could get one of those medical transport services?"

"I'm sorry Mr. Simmons but your wife is going to expire very shortly. Is there anything I could do to make this easier for you?" she consoled holding Wali's hands.

"Don't say that! My wife has never broken a promise to me in all of the twenty-some-odd years we've been married. She promised me that she will hold on until tomorrow....I'm sorry, I didn't mean to yell, but please, my wife asked me to do this one thing for her and if you don't help me. I will find a way on my own. I will carry her, if I have to." Wali was pacing back and forth.

"I understand...I will see what I can do....There will be papers for you to sign, because the doctor will never approve of her being transported in this condition. Secondly, your insurance will not cover you for something like this, because it is not approved by the doctor. ...," Rhonda explained.

"That's okay, I'll pay for it in advance. Find out what I need to do. My wife wants to go to church and I don't care what it takes to get her there."

"Okay Mr. Simmons....Don't worry. I will look into it and let you know what you have to do." Rhonda walked into the kitchen to use the phone.

"Kye are you okay?" Miles asked.

"I'm okay….this is just horrible."

"I'm here for you….I just want you to know that." Miles wrapped his arm around my shoulders to comfort me. My body was aching for him to entangle his body in mine. I don't know why, but that burning desire was rising up in me like Mount Saint Helens. I figured that some passionate, explosive and tantalizing sex would relieve me from all of this agony. Just for the moment, I needed to forget everything that has happened in my life. I needed Calgon (Miles) to take me away.

# CHAPTER 14
## *Sun Shine*

The nurse expected Benita to make her transition this evening between the hours of 7 and 8, but it was now half past nine and she was still holding on. Queen suggested that I go home and check on the kids. She didn't know that their father was there with them. I assumed she thought they were with Jamillah, my normal babysitter. At first I objected to leaving, but Miles also informed me that he needed to pick little Miles up from his mother's house and he would be glad to come back and get me when I was ready. Hmmm…. since when did he have little Miles during the week? Maybe he was picking Mile's mother up too. This was irritating me in my spirit. I did not want Miles to leave me. Not now, *not ever.*

I reluctantly left with Miles. Besides, Daddy was insisting that I get home and check on the kids. Daddy promised that if anything happened, they would call me immediately.

The entire ride back to the church I cried constantly. I was scared. I felt so helpless, like I was loosing everything around me….Benita….Miles….Kyasia….Leon and there wasn't anything I could do about it. Every now and then Miles would reach over and rub my thigh, "Kye, you aiight?"

"Yes," Upset or not, he better not play with me like that, because it only takes a rub on my thigh from the right guy to get this gravy train rolling.

When we got back to the church, Miles pulled up alongside my car to let me out.

"Kye, are you sure you're going to be okay to drive? 'Cause if not, I can get you home tonight and make sure you get back here to your car tomorrow," Miles offered.

"I'll be fine....Oh darn! In all the commotion, I left my bag inside....Do you mind coming in with me to get it real quick?"

"No doubt. Let me park the car."

Within minutes Miles and I were making our way through the pitch black hallway leading to my office. When we finally reached inside, the exit sign provided enough light for me to notice my bag sitting on Sandy's desk. What the hell! Why in the world was my bag doing on her darn desk?....that nosy so and so. I guess Benita is already passing the torch. I can't wait to check her on this tomorrow. Miles walked up closely on me from behind to check and see if I had found what I was looking for. Why did his body have to rub up slightly against mine?

"Miles, I just want to thank you for being there for me today. It really means a lot to me." I walked up close to him, looking him in the eyes.

"You know how we do. You're my dog for life. Yo', it ain't nuthin'." Miles looked down at me with that thugged out manly demeanor and I wanted him so bad I could taste it.

"You know at first I tried to fight the feelings I had for you. But now I realize that I can't...." I reached up and kissed him while wrapping my arms around his neck. He passionately kissed me back and suddenly the sun was beginning to shine in my life once again. I felt good for that moment....until he pulled away.

"Kye, we shouldn't...." was all Miles could say before I starting kissing him again.

"Miles, you know you want me....don't you baby?.... I know you want me...." I questioned while stripping seductively in front of Miles. As I unbuttoned my shirt and exposed my large full breast I questioned Miles, "You mean to tell me, that you don't want to touch these?" I proceeded to undo my belt and unzip my pants letting them fall to the floor. I was standing there with just my thongs on. "Miles I want you. I need you."

"Damn Kye, you holding like a mutha. But yo'...."

"Miles please!" I started unbuttoning his shirt and pulling down his pants. We were passionately kissing as we made our way down on the rug.

"Do you know how long I wanted to be with you?....." Miles said panting. I could feel his excitement growing larger and stronger between my thighs.

"Baby, you don't have to wait any longer." I kissed and licked all over Miles neck and chest. His body smelled like

Lever 2000 soap. Miles was caressing my butt and sucking on my right nipple as he was using his body to force my legs wide apart. Every time his manhood breezed past my love canal I gasped at the expectation. Just as his arousal was at it's peek, Miles stopped and his body fell completely on top of mine.

"Kye, I can't do this," Miles' sweat was dripping all over my face as his weight pinned my body to the rug.

"Why not?....you can't tell me that you didn't feel what I was just feeling." I started squirming my body trying to rekindle the fire.

"Damn...." Miles got up and starting gathering up his clothes.

"Miles! What are you doing?!" I couldn't believe that he left me naked on the floor.

"Look Kye! I've been trying to get at you for over 8 months now, and you wasn't trying to hear me....Yo', get up and put your clothes on!....We're not going there" Miles demanded. I was devastated. As I hurried to put on my clothes out of embarrassment, Miles continued.

"I'm getting back with Sonya, little Miles mother. We're really trying to make things work and I....I just don't want to do anything that will mess that up. Yo', look....you know, you'll always be my heart and no matter what I'll be there for you. For life, you can get that. You will always be my peoples." Miles held my hands forcing me to stand in front of him.

"I didn't realize that you was serious, all the times that you made indications that you wanted to get with me....But now.....I really love you...." I couldn't keep the tears from falling. I was broken hearted.

"Shhhh, I know....I love you too. But I'ma man, Kye.... and yo' look, I made a commitment to Sonya and I'm going to keep it. I'm in love with her and I'm going to do my part in making it work. Miles paused for minute. "You're a beautiful woman and your body is serious. Don't think a nigga wouldn't. If I did go there with you,....think about it, Kye? I wouldn't be any better than that dirty minister you was dealing with." Miles was referring to Leon and I knew he was right. But I didn't want him to get all philosophical on me right now. I needed him to make love to me and tell me that he wanted and needed to be with me. Instead he explained how he wanted to make his family work. Miles walked me to my car and reassured me that what had just happened wouldn't change our relationship.

As I rode home, Miles called my cell phone several times to make sure I was okay. In between calls I kept contemplating on the things Miles said about getting his family back together. The more I contemplated, the more I considered Michael as an option. Maybe God was trying to tell me to make things work with Michael. Maybe I should try and get my family back together.

When I walked in the house it was a quarter to eleven and the kids were sound asleep. Michael was sitting on the couch with his boxer shorts on, and nothing else; watching television. Talk about a ram in the bush. I rushed upstairs and took a nice hot shower. Wrapped myself in a towel and proceeded to unlock my room door, go inside, spray myself with body spray, rubbed my body down with sweet pea body butter. I slipped into a see-through Victoria Secret's shorts and tank top set. I was ready to hit the runway. I made my way downstairs and purposely went through the living room. I walked passed Michael yawning so that I would be perfectly arching my body as I allowed the glare from the television to illuminate my body as I paraded in front of him. Once I made it through the living room without him making an advance. I went into the kitchen and decided to get a glass of milk while planning my next move. As I raised my full glass of milk to my mouth ready to gulp it all down, Michael's unexpected hands grabbed my waist from behind caused the milk to spill all over the front of my body.

"Michael, wait…." I yelled

"No you wait!....." Michael demanded.

"Michael what are you doing!" I tried to resist.

"You know you want me to run up in that thing. Don't try to fight it." Michael was acting like an animal. The *dogism* in him was in heat. He licked the milk off my face. He sucked the milk off my breast, between my legs. He was panting as he turned my body around and pushed me hard up against the counter.

"Open up those legs…." Michael was pulling my shorts

down. He was wild. Ahhh,....he must have missed me something terrible. I couldn't get the shorts down good, before Michael plunged into me from behind. It was a good thing I was already wet, because the brother was fixed with hydraulics.

"Oooh......Oh....Ahhh!....." I moaned in ecstasy.

"Say my name....Girl....who's your daddy?" Michael was getting besidehimself. But as he lifted me onto the counter and spreaded my legs like butter and entered my oven with the tenacity of a ravaging stallion.

I responded, "You....Michael.....Oooh daddy, don't stop."

"Let's go upstairs?....." Michael was carrying me upstairs.

When we made it to the bed and locked the doors. We went at it like dogs in heat. It's a good thing the kids rooms were on the other side of the house. Afterwards, you could tell that Michael thought he was all in.

"I'm going downstairs to get something to drink. You want something?" Michael asked while sitting up on the side of the bed.

"No, but thanks for asking...."

"Okay, I'll be right back."

"For what! I hope you didn't think you was gonna sleep up here. Michael, having sex doesn't change anything.... Look, I will admit that I am seriously considering our family's future, but we still have a lot of things to work out. So let's just take it one day at a time....I will admit that tonight was a great start, at least, at trying to get to that point."

"No problem....Whatever you want." Michael walked downstairs. I got up and locked my door.

✤     ✤     ✤     ✤     ✤

It was the next morning when I realized that I didn't receive any calls regarding Benita. By the time Michael left with the kids. I was dressed and ready to go over to Wali's before heading down to the office, when Queen called and told me not to bother coming over to Wali's, because he had a transportation company bringing Benita to noon day service. I told Queen that instead of going to the office, I would just stay home and get some rest and meet them at the church a little before noon.

I put on the news and laid across my bed to take a nap. I must have dosed off when I heard the phone ringing.
  "Hello,"

"Yes, I'm trying to reach Mrs. Kiyah Payne," a very professional voice inquired. Wow, I haven't used my married name in over 2 years. Either it was one of those soliciting calls or a bill collector.

"This is she."

"Mrs. Payne, this is Sheila and I'm calling from First United National State Bank. This is a courtesy call to let you know that your account is overdrawn."

"What?!"

"Yes ma'am, your account as of right now, is $1,480.00 overdrawn," she explained.

"That can't be!....What about overdraft protection....My savings account should have covered that...." I panicked.

"I'm sorry ma'am, but you have a zero balance in your savings account."

"Stop playing. My paycheck was just directly deposited to that account two days ago. I should have at least $2000.00 in my savings. Oh no! More than that, I had the office Xmas club money in there as well....Excuse me, it should have been more than $10,000 dollars in that account. There must be a mistake."

"No ma'am, there isn't. We've been calling your home for the past few days inquiring about the unusual withdrawals you've been making from these accounts lately."

"What withdrawals?!"

"Let's see....on Monday, you withdrew your limit of $1,500.00 a day from your ATM card. Okay, and on that same day, you made a counter withdrawal for $3,000 from your savings account. On Tuesday, you withdrew another

$1,500 from your ATM card..."

She began to go into detail when out of pure panic I stopped her.

"Okay STOP RIGHT THERE! I never withdrew anything from an ATM on Monday or any other day this week....I don't even carry my ATM card with me on a daily basis.... Never mind, I'm on my way down to the bank to straighten this out." I slammed the phone down, grabbed my purse and I was out.

I made it down to the bank in a flash. I met with one of the customer care representatives, which explained thoroughly what the situation was with my accounts. There was nothing the bank could do, because the person or persons removing money from my account had the proper paperwork, slips and access information. It didn't take me long to figure out that this was the handy work of Michael. I couldn't believe it. I was going to kill that son of bi---. That sorry bastard had robbed me for over $12,000.00 and better than that, left me with over $1,400.00 in debt.  I had to rush home and go through all of my things to determine what else that sorry jerk had taken me for. I know I had to meet Wali and them down at the church by noon. But it was just a little after ten by now. I was shaken. What in the world was I going to do? I had checks coming into my account and didn't have enough money to cover them. What was I going to tell the people in the office about there Christmas money? Darn, I know I could stay in trouble. I was too mad to cry. I figured that maybe I could somehow replace the $8,000.00 before

Christmas. Who was I fooling? I can barely keep up with my own bills, let alone trying to set aside money for somebody elses. Now the tears were falling, because reality had set in. I was in a mess - so deep, that only God himself could get me out of.

When I reached the house, I noticed Michael's car already parked in the driveway. What was he doing home? I almost jumped out the car with the ignition still running. I was so anxious to confront him. I rushed inside ready to cut him. I was startled to a halt when I heard voices upstairs. I slowly and quietly shut my front door. Being careful not to be heard walking upstairs, I tip toed. The closer I got to the top of the stairwell, the easier it was for me to make out that the voices I heard were that of a man and woman moaning and groaning to art of lovemaking. I'm thinking should I go downstairs and get the butcher knife or should I call the cops on the nasty bastard? My nerves didn't wait for my brain to make a decision, because before I could gather my thoughts I was busting in my room and finding Michael going full throttle with some skanky, trashy looking broad.

"What the....!" I screamed.

"Kiyah! What are you doing here? You're suppose to be at work." Michael was stunned as he came to a halt still inside that hoe.

"How dare you!....Me?!....I thought you were supposed to be at work ....Michael you have went to far this time....But I guess the hours are very short when you're working your wife's bank accounts....Huh, Michael?....you sorry bastard!

I said taking off one of my shoes and throwing them at him. One caught him across the forehead. The other hit his whore in the chest.

"Kiyah! Stop it!" Michael hopped up from the bed.

"Don't tell me to stop it!....Where the hell is all of my money?"

"What money?,....Just calm down....."
I knew that low-life would never admit to what he has done. But that's okay....Because I'm sure it will come out in the wash.

"Michael, I swear to God if you don't get out of my sight right now....I'm going...." I threatened, throwing everything I could get my hands on, magazines, CD's, brushes, etc.

When Michael finally grabbed my hands to keep me from throwing anything else, I noticed that his little girlfriend had exited the building.

"Kiyah, can you just calm down....Look, I wasn't sure what you were going to do concerning us and...." Michael tried to explain.

"JUST SHUT UP! I can't stand to hear anymore of your lies Michael. I WANT MY MONEY BACK OR ELSE I WILL HAVE YOUR SORRY A—LOCKED UP!" I said pushing him.

"Kiyah, What are you talking about? I don't have your

money. How would I get your money? You're crazy. You better stop hitting me," Michael laughed, which only infuriated me. So I swung at him again and connected to his lower back as he was pulling up his pants,

"You know darn well what I'm talking about Michael. Why must you insist on lying? I guess I didn't just see you screwing another woman in my bed?" I screamed.

"What woman?" Michael taunted.

I couldn't take it anymore I tried to slap him across his face, but he stopped my arm mid - air and slammed me across the bed.

"Stop trying to hit me! I didn't take your damn money and I'm not going to let you keep hitting me. Now stop it!" Michael said pinning me down.

"Get off of me!" I kicked him square in the balls.

"You stupid bi---!" Michael yelled as he slapped me so hard across my face till it stung. I couldn't believe this punk had put his filthy hands on me. I had experienced one of Michael's beatings before. So I knew to calm down and get the deranged bastard out of my house. I'll let Shot Gun handle this one at a later date. "Kiyah, I didn't mean that.... you made me do it....I....I didn't take your money...." Michael was trying to get me to remove my hand from over the spot that he had connected his blow.

"I just left the bank Michael. The person withdrawing

money from my accounts had my deposit slips. My only deposit slips are kept in that night table over there. The person withdrawing money off of my ATM card, not only had the card, but the pin number as well. I always keep my ATM card in my night stand along with the rest of my banking information. The pin number was printed on the envelope I keep my card in….." I was making my point.

"Look, I didn't…."

"Oh, yes you did. I know you did, just like you broke into my room today to screw your little whore. You broke into my room plenty of times before to steal information. How could you do this to me? How do you expect me to be able to support our kids? It's bad enough that you don't pay me any child support, but then to go and rob me of what little I have…." I started crying all over again. "Just get out….Don't ever come back…." If I could have gotten his sorry behind locked up, I would have. But the bank manager explained that they do not involve themselves in matrimonial disputes. Because Michael and I were still married, they would not take action.

After Michael left, I was standing there in a daze not believing what I just experienced. When I sensed that my bedroom had a horrible funky smell. Even though I felt numb, I knew I had to sterilize this room, if I was going to ever sleep in it again. Just like Michael to go find some stinky chick. If I would have known he was still up to his old tricks, I would have never had sex with him without a condom. Now, here's something else for me to worry about.

It was ten minutes after eleven when I started cleaning and changing the sheets in my bedroom. As I was putting the old sheets in the garbage, I sighed with relief when I noticed the used condom. Thank God.

By quarter to twelve, I was checking my face in the bathroom mirror. It was all puffy from crying. I tried to cleanse it with witch hazel to get some of the swelling around my eyes down. It didn't work.

I pulled up to the church a few minutes after noon. The orderlies were wheeling Benita in. Wali was walking beside her. I parked my car and watched stunned at how in just a matter of weeks life has turned so completely around. At least a month ago, Benita was rolling around here, minding everyone's business. Benita looked at least 85 years old. She was only 53. Her head was limped over with her eyes shut. Her long gray hair was boyish short and pure white, matted in the back from laying in the bed so much. Wali looked like he could be her grandson. I was scared. For that one second, I totally forgot everything I was going through and mourned for Benita. I sat in my car thinking and crying. I was questioning God. "Why?....Why did you allow Michael to rob me of money that wasn't even mine? Was this my punishment for trying to fornicate in Your house? Or was it punishment for sleeping with a married man....Are you taking Benita from me, because I've done so many ungodly things? Lord, I know I've lost my way....But I tried so hard to do the right thing.... I'm tired of men using me. I'm tired of them lying and having motives. Lord, I know that You may not choose to answer this one request, especially since

I have not even tried to yield to Your will lately. But God, I feel like darkness keeps following me from one situation to another. Like, I've been searching for something with the lights off. Lord God, right now I need you to shine your light in my life once again. Lord I'm so messed up, that I don't even know what I need. I just need. Nothing feels right anymore. I no longer have any expectations or aspirations. My life is one big void....Lord, please send Your light and let it shine on me...."

The tears were rolling down so fast my hands couldn't catch them. I heard someone knocking on the car window.

"Kiyah, what's the matter?" It was Sandy.

"I'm okay,...."

"Girl come on....your whole family is looking for you.... Benita is asking for you," Sandy opened the car door helping me out and rushing me inside.

"Oh....let me hurry up...." I said running up the stairs that led to the sanctuary.

When I entered the sanctuary, Wali was bent down next to Benita. He had her hands. I walked up to them. Benita was gasping for breath. Everyone was quiet and standing around her. Suddenly I became angry.

"Why is everybody standing around her, like she's some sort of side show! Junior, why don't you get up there and have the choir sing a selection....Jared, Benita wanted to come to church....can we at least give her that?....this is not what she wanted...." I said crying. Jared started instructing everybody to go back to their seats and to go about service as usual.

As I was trying to get pass; Queen, Ev and Benita's two sisters to sit down, I felt somebody touch my hand. It startled me, when I looked around and noticed Benita struggling to reach for me.

"I'm here Bee," I said bending down and whispering in her ear.

"I..knew..you....straighten.....it.....out..Thank you......"
Benita face softened with a grin. She looked totally at peace.

Junior had the choir singing "Ordered" by Fred Hammond and Radical for Christ. This was one of my favorite songs. But not right now. They were already at the part where the lead singer was saying,
*"It may not feel good right now, but your steps are ordered....With tears in your eyes, help me say ordered.... you might understand it, but your steps are ordered...."*
Then the choir came in and sang the chorus, *"every step of a righteous man is ordered by God....even though you don't know his plight, he will reveal it all in time....Just know till then....your steps are ordered by God."*

Benita was relaxed and seemed totally at peace while the choir was singing this song. Again she forced herself to speak,

"I got........go........your the one.......Kye......I see da.....

light......shining........on you......."

I'm not the one, I'm too sinful to be the one. I haven't cleaned my act up enough to be the one.

"Benita, can you hear me?"

"Huh," she moaned.

"I'm not the one Bee. I was still sleeping with Leon and I'm so messed up emotionally I don't even know where to look to get peace in my mind."

"I knew.......All part......of.....God's plan....for....you...."

"God's plan? How can this be God's plan?"

"I love you......don't let me down Ki....yah.......let.... shine......Thank you.....Jes..us....huh....Jes...us.....Yes, Lord.....Yes....Lord....huh"

"Benita! Benita!" I cried. This was my first time seeing the life go out of somebody's body. Wali put his head against Benita's head and as I was trying to hug her I felt the dampness from his tears blending in with mine.

Rhonda pulled me back so that she could officially test her vitals and then she announced, "I'm sorry Mr. Simmons but your wife has made her transition."

"Don't be sorry. My wife is in a better place. Did you here what she was saying. She said, 'thank you Jesus and Yes Lord!'....She was walking into the presence of the Lord....

210

I'm going to miss you....but God needed you to be with him...." Wali said kissing Benita on the forehead as her body slumped over the wheel chair. The orderlies were preparing to move her over to the gurney. Everyone in the family wanted to say their good bye's as the choir belted out "Calvary".....

As my family and I followed the orderlies out with Benita's body, I noticed a familiar face sitting in the back of the sanctuary. It was Shyne. I was looking a mess - tore up from the floor up.

"I'm sorry, I forget you were coming over today....my sister-in-law....just passed and I just need to make sure my family is okay....so maybe today's not such a good time.... I'm so sorry," I apologized.

"No....Please, handle your business. Maybe I could help out?" Shyne stood up and walked over towards the aisle.

"Okay...wait, wait a second and I'll be right back."

I went outside and made sure that Wali was okay after the coroner took Benita's body away from the church. Queen insisted on Wali staying at her house, so she could assist him with making the arrangements. I wanted to tell my family how I was over $14,000.00 in debt. I needed to confide in my sisters about Michael. I wanted to lay my head on my brother's shoulder and tell him how another man had did me wrong. But I knew that for once in my life, I had to bear this cross on my own. A piece of our family's puzzle had just been lost and my problems weren't important right now.

After my family left, I tried to put on my game face. I went back inside the sanctuary where some of the choir members were still hanging around and talking about what just happened. Shyne was still sitting in the back patiently.

"I'm so sorry….maybe I shouldn't have invited you over here in the first place…..my life is such a mess right now…." I blurted out. I was overwhelmed with emotion.

"I know losing a family member is rough….Is there anything I can do?" Shyne consoled.

For some strange reason, I felt extremely comfortable with him.

"It's not just that. I found out today that my soon to be ex-husband just wiped out all of my bank accounts. I let him stay with me for a little while to make the kids happy, but he was going through my bank information and stole all of my money. I don't know why I'm telling you all of this?" I said shaking my head.

"No…that's aiight….look does this cat still have keys to your house?"

"Yes, I'm sure he does….That dog probably made a couple of spare sets."

"Okay, first thing we gone do is get a locksmith up there to change your locks," Shyne instructed.

"But I don't have any money for that." I explained.

"Don't worry about it....I think I could probably come up with a little sumthin'....Get them on the phone and I'll put it on my card."

Shyne paid for the locksmith over the phone and authorized them to charge any additional services needed after looking at the job in person. I really appreciated this from him 'cause I knew he really didn't have it like that. I just knew. First of all I didn't spot no car keys anywhere. Secondly, what kind of baller carries a credit card around.

After we sat outside the church and talked for awhile. I really got a sweet vibe from him. He seemed so sincere and honest. He explained that his car was in the shop so he caught a cab from Penn Station. Bingo! I'm good. I can always tell when a guy has loot and when he doesn't.

I offered to give him a ride back down to Penn Station. On the way down he asked if he could see me again. I knew instantly that I would. Even though Shyne didn't have a lot of money, I was seriously feeling his style.

After dropping Shyne off at the train station, I picked the kids up from school and headed over to Queen's house to assist her and Wali with Benita's arrangements.

After finalizing all of the arrangements, Queen reminded me that we had planned Kyasia's birthday party for Saturday. I expressed that maybe we should cancel it, in light of Benita's death. Wali was adamant that we should have

Kyasia's party in spite of the circumstances. He said that Benita would have wanted it that way. I, myself, had totally forgotten about the party. Reluctantly I consented to still having the party after Ev pointed out that Benita's funeral wouldn't be until next Thursday. Going on with the party would help to lift everyone's spirits.

Once we got that settled, I decided to run home and start making preparations. Besides, the locksmith was meeting me at the house at 7 p.m.

Making it through my doorway by 6:15, I checked the entire house and so far it seemed like Michael hadn't returned. The kids sat down as I explained to them that their daddy was no longer going to be staying with us. I didn't bother going into details. Kyasia seemed a little disappointed, but was comforted by the party plans we were now making. Unbeknownst to her, I needed to figure out how I was going to pay for this party.

By 7:30 the locksmith's had changed the front and back door locks and were on their way. Afterwards, the kids were watching television and I went upstairs to start sorting through my things. I was going through my bank information and suddenly all of the week events came crushing down on me.

All of my money was gone! Michael was screwing another woman in my bed. Oh God! How could all of this be happening to me? My mind kept spinning. Miles is in love with somebody else. Sean is gay. Benita is gone and Leon is still the same *grimey*, lying, manipulative bastard I knew a year and a half ago. My tears burned as they rolled over my face where Michael's fist struck me earlier. *That punk bastard hit me!* Wait till I tell Shot Gun about this. He's going to make that dog wish he had never been born.

I decided to take a nice long bath and try to relax.

After soaking for about an hour, Kyasia was banging on the door to get in.

"Mom, come on....when are you coming out?....Kaseem and I are waiting to take our showers. Your cell phone rang a couple of times too."

"Okay, I'll be right out." I said pulling my body up out of the water. I was physically and emotionally exhausted. I couldn't help but think about how Michael had violated me. That bastard! Just when I thought the tears had dried up. They were falling once again. I was mad as hell, I didn't want my kids to see me crying, but with Kyasia insisting on getting into the main bathroom, I could no longer hide it.

"Mom! Come on....it's after 8....Mom!" Kyasia yelled.

"Just a second....I'm coming!" I wrapped a towel around my body and opened the door.

"Mom, why were you in there so long?" Kyasia questioned.

"Relaxing honey....I'm sorry, I lost track of time."

"Mom everything's going to be okay....I know you're sad about Aunt Benita, so if you want, I can sleep with you tonight....just in case you wake up and need me to rub your back."

"That's okay, sweetie....I'll be okay. But thank you so much for being so considerate." I wasn't able to hold back the tears. "Ky...aisia....I'm going to go lay down in my room....Could you make sure your brother gets to bed?"

"Don't cry mom. I'll look after Kaseem for you. You go lay down and don't worry Daddy will come back...."

The only thing that worried me was that he would *try* to come back. If she only knew that her father was a lying, dirty, no good, scheming opportunist - she would flip. I dare not rob her of the image she has of her father.

I got into my nightgown, and checked my cell. I had 2 missed calls and 2 voicemails. One was from Miles. I listened. "Hey Kye! What's the deal? Just calling to see what's up. Sandy called and told me about Benita. So yo', I'm here if you need me. Holla!"
Beep....The next message was from Shyne.
"Kiyah, What's up Ma?....This is Shyne. I was just calling to see if everything was okay with you. I don't know 'bout you, but I felt like we connected immediately. Like we just vibed from the rip. Anyway, I enjoyed spending time with you today and if you need or feel like talking, hit me."

I decided not to call Miles back. Let him holla at his baby's mama. After playing Shyne's message over and over again, I decided to call him back.

We talked until I fell asleep.

I woke up Friday morning with the phone receiver laying on the pillow next to my ear. I had to smile as I put the phone back on the receiver. Shyne was so comforting and concerned. Last night we shared some of everything with each other. He told me that he lived in Manhattan on 89th and Lexington Ave. He swore down that he lived alone and was single. He gave me his home number, cell number and business number, which sort of motivated me to believe he was telling the truth. He worked for a packaging company and explained that he did alright (enough to pay the bills and have a little fun when needed.) I guess he sensed my concern when he divulged this information. I became very quiet. I liked Shyne, really I did, but I couldn't imagine being with another Michael.

At least Shyne did work and I felt a little better when later in the conversation. He explained that he was a man and that he wouldn't allow me to go in my pockets while I was with him. But by the same token - what he couldn't afford, we wouldn't have. This blew me away. I liked the way this man expressed himself.

I had to stop thinking about Shyne and get these party plans fine tuned. While in the process of doing that, I needed to call Random Access to pay the deposit for the dee jay. I grabbed my Visa from the nightstand to give them the number.

"I'm sorry Ms. Simmons, but your card was declined."

"That's not possible. I should have more than enough on that card….I don't even use it…..Okay, wait a minute. Let me get another card….hold on please."

"Sure."

"Okay, I'll put it on my MasterCard." I gave her the number. This was a brand new card, I had never used. It had a $2,500 dollar credit limit. I was saving it for Cancun, but now with Benita's death, there was no way I was going.

"Okay, thank you Ms. Sim…..Oh, I'm sorry ma'am but that card was declined also. Do you have any other form of payment?"

"DECLINED?!....This is bull---- . Look         I'm sorry. Is there anyway I could pay the full amount tomorrow when they arrive?" I was in shock.

"I'm sorry ma'am. But our policy requires that we have a deposit beforehand."

"Okay, okay. I'll bring you a cash deposit…Will $50 dollars be sufficient?"

"That's fine. We'll see you soon."

I'm going to kill Michael's a-- . On my way down to Random Access I decided to run through the hood and see an old friend. I needed a favor.

Friday had breezed by and I creatively came up with a way to make Kyasia's party happen without it costing me much money.

Queen was going to fry the chicken and make 10 lbs of potato salad; Ev was going to make a huge pan of baked turkey wings and macaroni and cheese. I decided to make a very large pot of cabbage. Sandy volunteered to do all the decorating. Sister Johnnie Mae from our church was baking the cake and Sister Moody was donating all the sodas. Once that was all settled, I thoroughly cleaned the entire house.

While cleaning, I found quite a bit of Michael's things. I put his stuff in two large garbage bags and sat them in the garage.

By 6:30 in the evening I was wiped out and in need of some rest. Kaseem was outside playing with his friends. Kyasia was in her room calling and confirming her guests for tomorrow.

I peeked into Kyasia's room.

"Excuse me honey, I'm going to take my shower and lay down. There's barbeque wings, rice and string beans on the stove. Can you make sure your brother is in the house by 7, gets cleaned up and eats? I'm going to bed. We have a big day ahead of us tomorrow."

"Okay mom, wait….Nisha, I'll call you back….okay?

Bye." Kyasia got off the phone. I'll take care of Kaseem for you....but Mom could you do me one big favor.....pleeeasse!"

"Sure, honey. What is it?"

"Mom, could Daddy come to my party tomorrow.... pleeeasse mom, pleeeasse?"

"Sweetie, listen....it's not a good idea for your father to come tomorrow....I'm so sorry honey....I would do anything for you.... But not that."

"Why?....You're mad at him, not me. It's my party. Not yours!" She ran in her room and slammed the door.

This is too much, if that little girl only knew. Her father just stole every dime we had, and almost jeopardized the very party she wants him to attend. How dare she be upset with me? I'm the one struggling to take care of her *by myself*. I'm the one that has spent my last dollar trying to make her party happen. She should be mad at him. He's the one living his life and not contributing a dime to hers. He's the one that walked away and only calls ever so often. I'm here - and always have been. But she longs for him and takes me for granted. That darn Michael, he's gone and still capable of hurting me. I could kill that sorry bastard if I got the chance.

I went into my room emotionally strained. I needed to talk to somebody. Anybody. I was going to call Shyne, but when I noticed that Miles had called again. I reluctantly called him back.

"Yo'," Miles answered.

"What's up. This is Kye….I see you called."

"Yeah, I did. What's up with you….You been acting funny lately. What's up wit dat?"

"I'm not acting funny. You acting funny. Besides I didn't want to bother you, especially while you're busy committing, being in love and everything." I was being sarcastic.

"Yo', you ain't right. That's messed up yo'. Look I'm not going to feed into all that. I was just checking on you. You still my peeps, but you buggin'." Miles was upset.

"Whatever, Miles. I'm tired. I'm about to go to bed. I just wanted to return your call…."

"Why you acting like that?! Yo'….what's wrong with you?!"

"I'm mad at you."

"What?!....mad at me?....How you gonna be, mad at me? I've always been straight up with you Kye. So how you gonna be mad at me? Yo' you ain't right….So you gonna do me like dat, huh?"

"You haven't always been straight up, nothing! You're a liar, just like your so called cousin."

"What?!"

"Yeah, I guess you don't remember telling me that after all of your baby mama's played you out while you were in jail, you said that you would never go back to them. Remember?....once you play me ain't no coming back," I taunted.

"Ooooh, so that's your problem. Yeah I guess you could get that. Well, if it's any comfort to you. Me and Sonya, we're just friends. It didn't work out."

"Aaawe, I'm so sorry Miles. What happened?" I pretended to be concerned. Deep inside I was ecstatic.

"It wasn't me, that's all I'm going to say. But for now, I'm just going to fall back."
Miles was hurt.

I eased up on him and talked until I saw the words Shyne flashing across the screen of my cell phone. It was on vibrate.

"Miles, I've gotta go.....but stop by Kyasia's party tomorrow.

"You got it....I'm out." Miles hung up.

"Hello,"

"What's up, gorgeous? It's Shyne."

222

His voice alone put me into another element. Instantly I felt peaceful, so peaceful that I fell asleep once again while talking with him on the phone. Was this a new habit?

## CHAPTER 15
### *Robbed*

Saturday was here and Kyasia was excited. I spent most of the morning doing her hair and helping her get dressed. She looked stunning. Wow, today my baby was officially a teenager.

The phone never stopped ringing. I talked with Shyne briefly off and on. But by 3 o'clock I was greeting guests and playing the perfect party hostess. Sandy did wonders decorating the house. Queen and Ev had the food under control. Sister Johnnie Mae and Sister Moody had delivered the cake and sodas over an hour ago. Everything was going well. The dee-jay showed up right on time. Thank God Miles came early and offered to pay the balance as a gift to Kyasia. He couldn't stay long, his job called him in for mandatory overtime.

By 4:30 the house was packed. There must have been over a hundred people there. Kyasia's gifts overflowed off the table and onto the floor. She was having so much fun. The kids were in the basement and my cousins and some of the other adults were sitting around the dining room talking. All of a sudden Michael walked in. I chose not to spazz out. I couldn't understand how he got in the house. I constantly checked the front and back doors to make sure they were locked. No one knew what was going on between us, so they just spoke, everyone - except Queen.

"I know you didn't invite that dog to the party. His lips

won't touch one crumb of the food my hands fixed," Queen whispered in my ear.

"I didn't invite him. He just showed up. You know Michael has a lot of nerve," I whispered back to Queen.

"Kiyah! Could I speak to you for one minute?" Michael asked.

"What Michael?" I walked over to him.

"I want to get the rest of my things."

"No problem. They're in the garage. Get them and get out!"

"Who do you think you're talking to?!" Michael yanked my arm and tried to pull me up the stairs. I was thinking, 'this nigga must be on drugs.'

"Get off of me Michael!" I was scared. Especially since he looked like a mad man and I had noticed a brand new shiny red axe in his right hand.

Ever Ready, Queen and my cousins rushed into the hallway where Michael had me choked up by my collar.

"Get off of her!" Ev screamed.

"Michael! You need to get out of here!" Queen screamed at Michael.

My cousin Don pried Michael hands from up under my chin. Queen helped me into the kitchen. She didn't sit me down good when we heard glass crashing like rolling thunder.

My family ran upstairs, where Michael had kicked down my bedroom door. He was slashing everything in sight. He had totally chopped my bed frame completely in half. The television, my dresser, the walls had huge gashes in them. Glass was everywhere.

When Michael looked up and saw me - he focused that demon on me, and lunged at me with the axe. My cousin Don stopped his arm, forcing Michael to fall backwards into the closet. But Michael still wasn't letting go of that axe. When I saw how relentless he was, I flew downstairs. Queen and Ev were on my heels.

"Call the cops!" Queen yelled into the kitchen.

"I WANT THAT B---- TO COME UP HERE NOW AND TALK TO ME!" Michael screamed from upstairs. "IF SHE DON'T COME UP HERE NOW, I'MA CHOP THIS MOTHA DOWN!" Michael was blacking out.

When some of the adult guests heard Michael's outburst they scrambled running downstairs and getting their kids and rushing them out of the house. Kyasia ran upstairs to see what was wrong. Some of her friends followed her. When she saw what her father was doing upstairs, she ran downstairs and straight outside crying. Queen tried to keep me in the kitchen, because she didn't want Michael to see me and try to attack me with that axe again. I forced my way out of the kitchen to run outside after Kyasia.

"What in the world is taking the cops so long?" Queen yelled as she was coming out the house behind me.

From outside I could here glass crashing. I didn't care about the house anymore. My little girl was devastated. She was laid out on the ground crying. I moved her friends out of my way, bent down and put my arms around her.

"Honey it's going to be okay. …."

"No, it's not!....It's all my fault!...Mom, I'm so sorry," Kyasia cried.

"Sweetie, this isn't your fault.…I don't want you to ever feel that way."

"It is!....I unlocked the back door for Daddy to come in…. He called earlier and told me to unlock the back door at 5 o'clock.…I'm so sorry Mommy.…I just wanted him to come to…."

"Shhhhh.…don't worry about it.…your father should have never asked you to do that.…It's going to be okay." I was now devastated myself.

"Okay my foot.…Kiyah you aught to whoop Kyasia's behind. She had no business doing what she did!" Queen chastised.

Before I could respond to Queen, I noticed the street was

flooded with cars of parents rushing to get their kids. Word had spread fast. The men in blue had came 5 cars deep and were entering the house.

As they were entering, Michael was coming out. Kyasia buried her face in my chest. She couldn't bare to see the cops handcuff and take her father away.

After they carted off Michael, we went back inside. I was horrified to find the entire second floor of my house demolished. Kyasia ran to her to her room hysterical in tears. That bastard trashed her room as well (not even caring that he hurt his own child in the process.) Queen had called Jared and Shot Gun - she wanted them to handle this. When they finally arrived, Michael was gone.

After my nerves finally settled down, I realized that I hadn't seen Kaseem since this whole incident had occurred. I looked all over and finally found him in the basement sitting in the corner with his faced buried in his hands crying.

"Kaseem….Baby, are you okay?....Come here."

"I thought you were dead," Kaseem hugged me tight. For the first time I realized that I was somebody's everything. He held me so tight that I could feel his need. He loved me, liked I loved my mother.

"Why would you think something like that?"

" 'Cause, all the kids was yelling and screaming -telling me your daddy is trying to kill your mother with a axe!....And I didn't want you to be dead….I don't want you to leave me," Kaseem cried.

"Baby….I'm never going to leave you….I promise….it's okay." I held him tight.

Kaseem and I went upstairs and found Queen and Ev trying to console Kyasia as she was trying to gather some of her things out of the debri in her room.

Sandy was downstairs trying to clean up. My cousin Don was outside talking with two of the cops that stayed around to ask questions. I didn't want to talk. I couldn't talk.

Queen demanded that the kids and I go home with her. She wouldn't be able to rest with us here after what just happened.

I told her to take the kids with her. I would be okay. I needed to try and straighten up this mess. Queen was adamant, but when Don told her that the cops said that Michael would be in jail until at least Monday (when he will go before a judge) she finally agreed to let me stay.

Sandy was the last one to leave; Ev dropped her off.

Thank God, I really wanted to be alone. I was embarrassed, ashamed and distraught.

I went upstairs to my bedroom to see what could be salvaged from the mess that Michael had created. Wow, I'm a mother and right now I needed my mother badly. If she was living nothing like this could have ever happened. It's amazing that the lost of her presence alone had such a great impact on our family. It's almost has if she took our covering with her.

I wanted my mother so bad I could go and dig up her grave.

I felt like someone had tore my heart out, as I fell on my knees to start picking up the plastic pieces from broken CD's. I noticed a Yolanda Adams CD that seemed to be unharmed. Grabbing my portable CD player out of the closet, plugged it in and put it on. Within minutes her voice rang through the room singing. *"Quietly, He speaks to me, gently, He leads me. Lovingly the shepherd carries me. He carries me hidden safely in His bossom. I feel His love inside, when other times my friend - I couldn't. He knows just what's best for me. He knows just what I need."* I hadn't listened to this CD in over a year. I know it was nothing but the hand of God that allowed this one CD to be saved. The words were cutting through me like a butcher's knife. I felt right then, like that song was written specifically for a time like this. I was so broken and burnt out about what has happened, but never stopped to think that I could have been dead. Only God, kept Michael from using that axe when he had me alone in the hallway. The tears were streaming down as Yolanda continued, *"I'm so glad that He knows, He knows just what's best for me....The good shepherd knows, yes He knows. Just what I need.... Quietly. He speaks. Gently. The Master leads. So lovingly, He carries me to a safe place of rest and I feel the Master's* **unconditional** *love...***Everlasting** *love, ever so deeply inside of me...I'm so glad Jesus knows.. Jesus knows... just what's best for me...."* As Yolanda sang I felt God's forgiving power filling the room. I could feel myself approaching His throne of grace. I was ready to wash all of my dirty laundry in God's sea of forgetfulness. I felt the anointing in Yolanda's voice as she belted out the last verse, "*I'M SO GLAD JESUS KNOWS JUST WHAT'S BEST FOR ME AND MY HOUSE....WE SHALL, PRAISE HIM FOREVER...THE GOOD SHEPHERD KNOWS...yes, He knows....YEAH THOUGH I WALK THROUGH THE VALLEY OF THE SHADOW OF DEATH....yes, He knows... I WILL FEAR NO EVIL..FOR JESUS IS WITH ME...yes, He knows....HE LEADS ME HE GUIDES ME, IN THE SHELTER OF HIS ARMS HE HOLDS ME....yes, He knows. The good shepherd knows just what I need.*" Right then I knew that God was telling me to surrender. Before today, this song had never affected me this way. I felt the need to repent.

"Lord, I need You now like never before....Father, I give up....I don't want to try it my way anymore....I'm sorry God. I thought I could ease my hurt, disappointment and pain with the company of men and Lord. That desire has only caused me more pain, disappointment and hurt....I don't know who I am anymore....Oh God! I'm scared; all these changes I've been going through, HAS CHANGED ME....All I do is cry....sometimes I don't even know why I'm crying....I'm a failure; I've failed as a wife, I'm failing as a mother and even when I failed you, God; You still have mercy on me. I could have been dead or just another statistic, but You didn't see fit to let none of those things be....If You don't do anything else for me God, I want You to hear me, one more time, so I can say 'thank You' ....I don't know if you choose to hear me, but if you...."

"I HEAR YOU KIYAH!"

I jumped. Was I loosing it? Simultaneously, the phone rang.

I wiped away my tears and answered.
  "Hello,"

"Sweetheart, I know you probably don't want to hear from me, but...." It was Leon, "....The Holy Spirit just dropped you in my heart so strongly that I just *had* to call."

Would God use *Leon*? After explaining my catastrophe to Leon, he eagerly came and picked me up. He insisted on putting me up in a ritzy hotel in New York City. He said the ride would be good for relaxing my nerves. Without objection, I went. I needed to get away. Leon was really going out his way to comfort me.

I was pleasantly shocked when Leon prayed with me, gave me a wad of cash and left.

It felt like heaven when I lowered my body in the hot and steamy Jacuzzi filled with bubbles. I didn't bother packing a bag so I climbed into the cool sheets wearing only my birthday suit.  Snuggling up underneath the covers, I fell fast asleep.

✤　✤　✤　✤　✤

"What the Hell!" Leon had scared the daylights out of me.  He had un-expectantly climbed his nasty, naked self into my bed and was trying to enter me while I was asleep. I struggled to get away from him. As I was fighting to get out of the bed, Leon continued to grab me. How dare he use a situation like this to *rob me without a gun*? This nigga' thought he was entitled to this. Oh hell no! His money isn't long enough and his sex was no longer strong enough to make me feel cheap again. It wasn't until I clawed his face that I was finally able to break free. Pulling away, I ran into the bathroom to put my clothes back on. While putting on my clothes, I peeked out of the bathroom and noticed Leon examining the damage I had inflicted on his face. This was my chance. I came out the bathroom and began to run straight out the door. Leon yelled after me, but I ignored him and kept running. I didn't want any parts of him. I was determined not to go back down that road again. Now I'm out here in the middle of New York City with no money and nowhere to go.

What was I going to do?

If only Miles were here. I know he would hold me down. He always does.

I was so distraught and tormented that I didn't care how openly I cried. But thank God, the diva in me rose up and I put on my Gucci shades.

Being disoriented, it was 1 a.m. when I realized that I was approaching the corner of 89th and Lexington Ave. As I prepared to ring Shyne's bell, I wondered how he was going to feel about my little surprise visit. But I was desperate. Buzzzz!

"Yeah,….Who is it?" Shyne's voice came through the

233

intercom.

"It's me....Kiyah....I....I...."

"Come on up...." He buzzed me in right away. Shyne met me as I made my way down the hall towards his apartment. I didn't have to say a word. He stretched his arms out and I fell into his warm embrace. As he guided me into his apartment, he whispered "I got you....everything's going to be okay."

After Shyne made sure I was completely comfortable, he ran out to get me something to eat. While he was gone, Miles called my cell. Sandy had informed him on what happened back at the house. Miles was furious and insisted on coming to get me.

✢    ✢    ✢    ✢    ✢

It's a year later and Benita's words still burn in my mind, "let....shine...." Those were her last words to me. Even on her death bed, God was using her to deposit into my life.

It's amazing. I can't believe I'm sitting here staring at this 5 carat platinum, princess cut, diamond ring with baguettes, *shining* on my finger. He proposed to me. I wonder....

# Robbed

## By Dy-Shawn Simpkins & Deborah Smith

Over and over again
The enemy has **Robbed** me - without a gun,
Enticing me with worldly desires
That, from afar seem fun
Searching for satisfaction
The end result - there was none.

Every day, every second it happened;
**Robbing** me of my integrity and pride
Utilizing things that appealed to the naked eye
Money, cars, expensive clothes and sexual desires

That's when the **Robbery** begun and
The gun was no longer needed

How far have you gone?
How low have you stooped?
What was the amount of money?.......
That caused you to be Robbed without a gun.

Everyone has a price
To be bought and even sold
WHAT IS YOUR SELF WORTH?
Like it or not  - we have all been **ROBBED**.

There is none righteous, no not one
For all have sinned and been
**Robbed** without a gun.

But fear not, all is not lost
Christ paid the price
To restore all that was stolen
If you put your faith in Him
You will no longer continue to be
**ROBBED!**

# Dedication

To my Lord and Savior Jesus Christ: *'Your grace and mercy have truly brought me through. I'm living this moment because of YOU.'* In you I have found myself, and through you I will continue to edify humanity while glorifying Your Name. Your praise will always be in my mouth and in my writing.

To my children, Kindness and TJ: When I look at all of the gifts that God has given me, you both are by far my greatest treasures. I live to be an example of how you can achieve any dream, no matter how big. I love you unceasingly and unconditionally.

In memory of my dear Mother, Evangelist Constance B. Smith: Neither words nor deeds could ever express the admiration and appreciation to my Lord and Savior Jesus Christ for giving me the gift of life through such an awesome woman of God. Mommy, I Love You.

To my Dad, Bishop Willie L. Smith Sr.: You are and always will be the most respected businessman I know. Thank you for being the type of father that most men can only aspire to be. I will always believe in you because you've always given me reasons to, time and time again. I love you.

To My Brothers and Sisters: Willie, Victor, Bernard, Lori, Jerry and Tyrone: Thanks for all of your support throughout the writing of this book, as well as all of my life's endeavors. Being the baby sure has its perks when you are blessed with sibling like you.

To My Sister, Roberta: You hold an extra special place in my heart in that you have been like a second mother to me; even more, my best friend. Thank you for your encouragement, guidance and commitment. I could not have found the peace of mind to release this second project without your faith in it.

To the love of my life, Dy-Shawn Simpkins: Though there may be rain, you are the sunshine and serenity that has helped this flower to bloom. I only hope to match the dedication to our life and love that you have shown to the world and me. The air is so sweet when you are around. Everything is coming up roses!

# Acknowledgements

I am deeply appreciative to all of the wonderful people who have helped to make my second novel possible:

To my publicist and manager, Najiyyah Brooks Harris of True Vine Marketing & Public Relations. Thank you for your genuine spirit, integrity and diligence in the shaping of my career. I will forever be grateful for your professionalism and loyalty. I look forward to many years of us working together.

To Joanie Smith, my very talented and determined editor. Thank you for the countless hours of reading, editing and challenging me to be the writer God created me to be. I look forward to many more books being born with your help.

To Al-Saadiq Banks of True 2 Life Productions, author of *'No Exit'*, *'Block Party'* and *'Sincerely Yours,'* thank you for being real in your writing and in your living. I look forward to a collaborative effort one day!

To KaShamba Williams author of *'Blinded'*, *'Grimey'* and *'Driven'* and Mark Anthony author of *'Paperchasers' and 'Dogism'*, for being part of this great movement of urban writers! I am grateful for your input and belief in my project. Keep writing those bestsellers, I'm right behind you!

To my friends, church family (CPC) and loved ones, because I have received the greatest amount of prayers and support from you!

Shout outs to: The 611 crew (Hill Manor); Vanessa, thanks for being such a true and good friend. Big Meek, J.O.E., Rev, Nicole, Salaam, Fee, Mootsie;

Selene and Robert Haskins, Barbara Weeks Johnson, Flo (you still my lil sis), Beverly Smith, Nicole Camacho, Kevin Brown and all of CPC daycare staff. Monique Singleton, Sybil's hair salon, Tamika and Taniesha and the staff at Trax the Weave Station, Henry (L.A. perfection nails).

To the Simpkins Family: Mommy (Brenda), who could ask for a better mother in law, I love you.
Sha-miel and Kelli, Twauny, J.R., El-Juan, Grace, George and Dina, Aunt Sheila and all of the Simpkins family; Thanks for your acceptance and support – I love you all!

Shout out to Johnny and his wife Nicole;

My nieces and nephews: Co-Co, Chanel, Jahmaah, Jerell, Jaliel, Alliah, Mook, Boo-boo, Mama, Levar, Maurice, Le'Aja, Romell, lil Mel, lil Vic, lil Willie, Tamara, Taheerah, Nandi, Te', Jaliyah, Aja, Mya, Tee- Tee, Zahir and Phat daddy.

# DEBORAH SMITH PUBLICATIONS
## ORDER FORM

1051 Stuyvesant Avenue, #319
Union, NJ 07083
**www.deborahsmithonline.com**
info@deborahsmithonline.com
**1 (888) 698-8486**

### _Robbed Without A Gun_
**ISBN # 0-9746136-9-X**          **$14.95**
**Sales Tax (6% NJ)**                    **.89**
**Shipping/ Handling**
**Via U.S. Priority Mail**          **$ 3.85**
**Total**                              **$19.69**

**Also by the Author:**
### _Ministers With White_
### _Collars and Black Secrets_
**ISBN # 0-9746136-0-6**          **$ 9.95**
**Sales Tax (6% NJ)**                    **.60**
**Shipping/Handling**
**Via U.S. Priority Mail**          **$3.85**
**Total**                              **$14.40**

### _Sex Secrets_ - _For the Married Woman_
**ISBN # 0-9746136-1-4**          **$ 9.95**
**Sales Tax (6% NJ)**                    **.60**
**Shipping/Handling**
**Via U.S. Priority Mail**          **$3.85**
**Total**                              **$14.40**

## PURCHASER INFORMATION

Name: _____

Address:_____

City:_____ State: _____

Zip Code: _____

Robbed Without a Gun: (QTY) ___

Ministers With White Collars and Black Secrets:
(QTY) ___

Sex Secrets - *For the Married Woman*: (QTY) ___

HOW MANY BOOKS? _____

Make checks/money orders payable to:
**Deborah Smith**
**c/o Deborah Smith Publications**

*We also accept all major credit cards by phone or web.*